Tales from the Job Site
A Frustrated Contractor Confesses

By
Michael A. Pesola

PublishAmerica
Baltimore

ISBN: 1-4241-5787-0
PUBLISHED BY PUBLISHAMERICA, LLLP
www.publishamerica.com
Baltimore

Printed in the United States of America

This book is dedicated to my father and mother, Jack and Marie, who through their guidance and love have given me the tools necessary to succeed in life. Every day that passes only makes me realize how fortunate I am.

Acknowledgment

Many thanks to my loving wife Sara who tirelessly processed this book on the computer and offered prudent advice when needed.

Foreword

These stories are not meant to offend anyone. They are written merely to enlighten the reader to the intricacies of remodel work. Remodeling has long since overtaken new construction in dollars spent; therefore it stands to reason that many contractors and homeowners out there have a story to tell. These stories can take many forms, from horror, to comedy, to yes, even success stories.

My father taught my brothers and I most of what we know. He instilled in us a moral code that helped us to distinguish right from wrong and he taught us how to do things right the first time. God bless him, he is still with us teaching and guiding, albeit more now by example and nuance.

My father used to say to me, "Son, I've forgotten more than you've already learned." As I think back on those words, they couldn't ring more true. In our business, as in life, several truths are clear:

The remodeling business is a constant learning process.

The remodeling business can be equally stressful for the homeowner and the contractor.

Remodeling is like a chess game. Anyone can move, it's finishing that counts.

If you're going to do something—anything—do it right.

In the end, if these stories entertain you or provoke some thought during your remodel project, or if you can find some humor in the whole process, then I guess the book was worth it.

Michael A. Pesola

Introduction

Much has been made over the years about the sorry state of general contractors; their abuses, their bad name, etcetera, etcetera. It has been widely reported in television exposés, newspapers, and magazine articles that contractors lack integrity and are responsible for numerous atrocities in the world including, but not limited to: overcharging the customer; receiving large draws and then abandoning the job; sloppy work; creating leaks and mold; instigator of any malfunctions in the home, including drywall cracks and broken appliances; and use of low-quality products. I'm sure you get the picture. (If you don't you must be living in a vacuum, or you frequently take on water in a very dark place with rich soil … like a mushroom.) Anyway, the funny thing is that many contractors go totally unreported. You don't hear about them unless some client talks about the great quality work they performed or how they completed a project on time. These contractors don't even have to advertise! These are the contractors that this book is written for. The following stories all reflect the contractor's view on a profession that is taxing, complicated, and never boring.

Let me transport you to a nearby planet where five contractors can bid a project and no two bids will be close in price. Come with me to a world where husbands and wives argue about a project when only one of them even wanted to start. A strange world where red can be green, and linoleum costs the same as marble tile. Many times on this world one gets the feeling of being watched, perhaps by visitors from another planet, filming us for their version of a dysfunctional reality show.

If these stories sound familiar, remember, you're not alone out there.

Author's note

This book of short stories is a work of fiction. Names, characters, places, and incidents are the product of the author's imagination or are used fictitiously.

Any resemblance to actual events, locales, or persons living or dead is coincidental.

—MP

Contents

Chapter 1
Oil-Rubbed Bronze

A few years ago we were remodeling a bathroom for a nice lady using high-end plumbing fixtures—a state-of-the-art spa, beautiful expensive porcelain tile, and a 3/8-inch-thick glass frameless shower door.

In a bathroom remodel, some of the last items installed are the plumbing fixtures, such as the sinks, faucets, toilet, the shower controls, and the showerhead. The sink faucets, shower valve, and showerhead in this case had what the manufacturer called an "oil-rubbed bronze finish" and the four pieces combined cost over $900.

After the fixtures were installed the plumber turned on the mixer valve control and ran some water through the showerhead to test it. The next day the owner asked me to come into the bathroom. She pointed at the mixer valve control under the showerhead where there were what appeared to be water spots on the bronze finish (obviously caused by drips from the showerhead above) and said, "What can we do about these spots, Mick, they look horrible?"

I replied, "Quite frankly I don't know, Mary, we've never installed products with this type of finish before. I'll call my plumbing supplier and get a phone number for the manufacturer and see what they say."

After a few calls I reached the manufacturer and asked what the process was for removing these water spots. My thinking was (1) it was obvious the fixtures would have to get wet at some point, and (2) there must be a manual or instructions for caring for such an expensive investment. After all, why pay that kind of money for a product that spotted so easily?

Not so. The company rep explained that this was a hand-rubbed finish and one should avoid getting the fixtures wet. Incredible! I wondered what would happen when Mary washed her face for the first time and then turned off the faucet with wet hands.

I asked the rep, "How are you going to keep water off a valve that is directly under a showerhead, not to mention splashing off someone's body?" but I received no good answer. To make a long story short, Mary learned to live with her bronze fixtures.

"Maybe," she said, "these fixtures are only supposed to be for show and not for actual use." (Another case of learning by experience.)

Chapter 2
Ride 'Em Cowboy

A few years ago one of my brothers was preparing to solder a mixer valve and showerhead in a customer's bath. As is the custom with many plumbers, all the copper was dry fitted together with the valve and the showerhead piece in place. This would ensure a good fit prior to the more permanent soldering of the pipes. The customer, Al, as was his fashion, hunkered in close to my brother in the confines of the bath, looking over his shoulder. After my brother had finished the preparations, he walked into another room to get some soldering equipment. When he returned he found an empty void where the valve had been sitting. The customer, Al, a highly inquisitive fellow, had removed it and was studying the fixture in another room.

Much later in the day after my brother had shared this unique episode with me, I approached Al's wife.

"Sally," I said, "do you mind if we purchase a saddle for this project?"

She look puzzled, "Why, whatever for?"

"So we can strap it on my brother Tony's back so Al can ride him around the job."

Sally was silent for a good ten seconds; not a good sign.

Finally, she burst out laughing, "That's my Al!"

Message delivered.

Chapter 3
Don't Tell Me What I Said

Often at the beginning of a workday I dole out directions or instructions to the lead men. Usually I make diary notes or scribble them on my weekly schedule sheet. I trust my memory, but I think I'll always be a "paper person." Periodically I would check on a particular employee to see the fruits of his labor under my direction. From time to time it became apparent that in some instances, the work wasn't being completed to my specifications. On this particular morning I had just finished telling Joe what was wrong with his work. What follows is a loose translation.

"Mick, you didn't tell me that."

"Yes, I did, Joe."

"Mick, you never told me that!"

"Joe, don't tell me what I said. I know what I said and I'll be the first one to tell you when I'm going senile!"

Very soon after this conversation I started giving my daily instructions in writing—and keeping a copy for myself. Needless to say, cases of memory lapses have gone down dramatically. Both theirs and mine.

Chapter 4
My Cabinets Are Turning Yellow

Some jobs run so smoothly I almost have to wonder why I'm getting paid. Well, maybe I'm embellishing slightly. The job I am thinking of was a large addition/expansion and a state-of-the-art kitchen remodel totaling over $300,000 back in 1999.

The couple, who we will call Bob and Carol, are delightful people and I share a warm relationship with them to this day. Under the best of circumstances it is hard enough to complete an extensive remodel when the house is unoccupied. In this case, the couple and their son chose to live in the house during the remodel.

Nevertheless, for six months my men and subcontractors co-existed in relative harmony with this family. Through dozens of decisions, temporary plastic walls, a refrigerator used on the back porch, and Bob's small office, which served as the temporary kitchen, the job progressed as smoothly as could be expected in such trying conditions.

When the project ended I completed a walkthrough with Bob and Carol, went over the final billing, and received a check with much thanks. Because of Bob and Carol, we were gearing up to start another project two houses down the street—they had highly recommended us and I thanked them for that.

About two weeks later I received a call from Carol. She said that the cabinets in the bathroom were turning yellow. This gave me great pause, because, if true, it could be a costly and time-consuming repair. Even if the cabinets had "yellowed" I couldn't understand how it could have happened in such a short period of time. The bathroom was large with panels on the side of the spa, two seven-foot vanities, a make-up counter, and a large hutch all expertly painted by my painting subcontractor.

Expecting the worst, I told Carol I'd meet her the next day. We exchanged pleasantries and then walked into the new bathroom. At first glance I saw nothing wrong. The phone rang and Carol, pointing toward her vanity, said she would be right back.

I looked at the face of the vanity and still saw nothing wrong. I opened a few drawers and again saw nothing unusual. Then I opened the doors below the sink and saw what appeared to be a yellow film lining the inside walls of the cabinet. Now *that* was unusual!

Then I noticed some kind of hair-curling apparatus. The lid was off and it was plugged into an outlet on the back vanity wall. Apparently this appliance had been working with the cover in the raised position spraying whatever solution was inside of it onto the surrounding cabinets.

Carol was embarrassed when she saw the cause of the yellowing. I on the other hand was extremely thankful that it was not the large cabinet problem I envisioned. It is easy to make assumptions in this business and sometimes, as in life, those assumptions are incorrect even by the most well-intentioned people.

Chapter 5
Check Your Ego at the Door
or I Always Thought My Eyesight Would Go Before My Hearing

This story comes under the "too close to home" category. My wife and I had recently moved into a new home built on a concrete slab floor in Davis, California. Much of Davis is built over fertile soil once used for farming. Consequently there is a fair amount of settling of the slabs under homes built in this area, resulting in concrete and drywall cracks.

One night after a long day of phone calls and customer meetings, my wife mentioned to me that the floor in the master bathroom is warm. I told her not to worry about it, it's probably coming from the skylight. She persisted, "Duh, it's not from the skylight!"

"Look, girlie, who's the contractor here? Don't worry about it. There's nothing wrong." (I love my wife, but after all who's the expert here?)

A month went by after this conversation. We had just received our second water/sewer bill from the city. I was in shock! The first bill we received two months ago was high enough, but I attributed it to the high cost of living in Davis versus where we formerly lived in Sacramento, in a municipal utility district.

This bill literally forced me on my hands and knees, working my hands over the linoleum in front of the vanity on the bathroom floor. Sure enough, it felt like we had radiant heat under the flooring similar to what we added in so many customers' bathrooms. The only problem was, this bath had never been remodeled and I don't even know if radiant heat was available in the early seventies, when I was still in high school.

As it turned out, there was a broken hot water pipe under the concrete slab. As an added benefit, this leak raised my "metered" water bill into the vicinity of a mid-sized monthly car payment.

Several years have passed since this unfortunate incident. As a form of penance my wife now has a newly remodeled bathroom with an additional hundred square feet of space … and low-voltage radiant heating under the new tile.

The moral of the story is that you should always pay attention to your wife, and pay closer attention to wives who walk around barefoot.

An interesting side note: My insurance company paid for most of the damage, except for the two dollars' worth of copper pipe that failed. (Bizarre!) When I suggested to them that we might as well replace the last few feet running towards the shower, they said they couldn't do that until the pipe failed. (Even though it was inevitable and would have saved a great deal of money.) Go figure.

Chapter 6
You Know You've had Enough When:

• You send a man to do apartment maintenance at 10:00 a.m. in a college town and they have to step over ten lifeless bodies passed out on the floor to do their work in a two-bedroom apartment.

• Your maintenance man has to continually fix the floodlight by the pool on warm spring or summer days.

• Your eighty-three-year-old male customer walks around the house naked in front of you and all your employees … and gravity has done a thorough job.

• You wake up in a cold sweat when rain starts pelting the skylight over your bed.

• A customer blames you for drywall cracks fifty feet away from the kitchen remodel work.

• Your customer calls you because she has hot water running in her newly replaced toilet???

• You enter your customer's house to start work, he calls you into the bath under construction (the one with no walls), and he is sitting there naked, on the toilet, with a newspaper in his hand, casual as can be, ready to discuss the location of his showerhead!!!

• Your employee calls in with the flu on Monday and is ready to go back to work on Tuesday. (I like a fast healer. I wonder why this always happens on Monday?)

• Employees call in sick when they know they will be digging trenches or pouring concrete in ninety-degree weather.

• You are standing in a small bathroom talking to your lead man and the plumber. Your customer walks in and says, "I've got to get going! This place is overrun with authority."

Chapter 7
Dessert

I was meeting a customer at her house to go over her final contracted payment. When we finished going over the invoice, she handed me a check and we shook hands. Something was bothering her though, and I soon found out what it was.

"Mick, there is something I have to tell you." We both sat back down at the table, the gravity of the situation pulling me down into my chair.

"What is it, Betty?"

"Well, you have to promise you won't tell."

Well, there's a first, I thought. "Okay, I won't. What is it?"

"Well, one of my daughter's fudgesicles was missing from the freezer this morning."

"What?" was all I managed to say. I was taken by surprise. I was expecting maybe a scratch in the linoleum or a request for a paint touch-up, but ice cream?

"My daughter loves fudgesicles," she went on steadily. "Every morning the first thing she does is count how many fudgesicles are left in the box. She has one every afternoon."

"I don't understand. Are you saying that one of my men opened up your freezer and ate a fudgesicle?"

"No, it wasn't one of your guys, but I know who did it."

My consternation was slowly turning into a mild form of anger. As she spoke I tried to calculate the audacity it would take an employee to actually open up a customer's refrigerator, and then have a nice little snack. Snapping out of it, I asked, "Who was it?"

"It was your cultured marble man."

"You've got to be kidding! How do you know?"

"Well, he was the only one in the house besides us, and my husband doesn't eat ice cream."

"Betty, this is extremely embarrassing. I don't know what to say, but I do know what I'm going to do. I'm going to call the marble guy's boss and let him know what happened. I can't have this kind of thing going on in my customer's homes."

As I finished my little speech, Betty's eyes met mine. They were smiling and pleading at the same time.

"Please don't say anything, Mick. I don't want to get anyone in trouble."

"Betty, if I don't say anything, he'll never know and he may do it again."

"If he wanted the fudgesicle that bad, let him have it."

We eventually shook hands and I left, perplexed. To this day I have never brought this story to the attention of the individual who would most benefit from it. Fortunately, as far as I know, the ice cream bandit has not struck again.

Chapter 8
The Road to Nowhere

One morning I was driving back from the Building Department to my office when I noticed our truck and trailer parked along the side of the road on 7th Street.

Since I write all the estimates and meet all potential customers, it would stand to reason that I would remember all of our job sites, especially current ones. The job on this street however, was drawing a blank.

After spacing out for what seemed like a couple of minutes, I beeped up my partner Mark and asked him if we had a job going on 7th Street. After a pause that seemed to convey maximum ignorance on my part, Mark said, "Not that I know of," with a snicker.

Next I paged our employee Bob, who was driving the truck and trailer that day. The conversation went something like this:

"Bob, Mick here. What do you have going right now?"

"I'm on my way to the dump," Bob states with authority, and not the slightest hesitation.

"Okay, Bob, call me when you're done."

"Ten-four."

Now, I don't mind a guy taking a break now and then. I draw the line however, at paying people to sit at home watching *Oprah*

Winfrey. Fortunately for us this was an isolated incident. Most of our employees actually work the eight hours they are paid.

What a concept!

P.S.: Bob is no longer with us.

Chapter 9
Tom, Are You Sure?

One of my first estimates after I became a licensed general contractor was a bid to remove the existing plywood siding on the back of a two-story home and replace it with cedar sidewall shingles.

I measured all the wall area footage, subtracted windows and added five percent for waste. After figuring in labor and overhead costs I came up with a total and gave the owner my price.

A week later the owner accepted my proposal and I proceeded to line up the materials we would need to complete the work. In the lumberyard I found the sidewall shingles. These particular shingles came stacked tight in boxes. I glanced at the box and saw that one box covered one square, or 100 square feet. I had calculated that we would need just under 1,400 square feet, so I loaded fourteen boxes into the truck and brought all the material to the job site.

The following week my brother Tom started the project. It was slow going because much of the work had to be done off of a scaffold. Fortunately I had factored that into our bid and allowed enough man-hours (labor) to cover our costs.

On the second day late in the afternoon, I received a call from Tom.

"Mick, we're just about out of shingles."

How can that be, I thought? "How many are you short, Tom?"

"It looks like about fourteen boxes, Mick."

"Fourteen boxes! Are you sure, Tom? Oh, I get it. Nice joke, Tom. You had my heart pumping there for a second."

"I'm not joking, Mick. We're just about halfway up the building."

I was perplexed. I remember measuring and then re-measuring to double-check my figures. My father always said to measure twice and cut once. This mantra saved me from many mistakes in the past, but it didn't help this time.

I drove out to the job site and soon discovered my mistake. On the side of each box were the words "covers one hundred square feet." The words following though were the words that hurt ... "Fourteen inches to the weather."

When these shingles are applied you start on the bottom row and work your way up horizontally. Each row overlaps the preceding row. A typical overlap would be between six to eight inches, sometimes a little less, sometimes a little more. On our customer's home, the existing shingles were set about seven inches to the weather.

I have seen and worked on countless homes with cedar shingles, especially on the east coast. To this day I have never seen them applied at fourteen inches to the weather. In fact, if applied in that fashion, aesthetically, it is not pleasing and, for waterproof and wind protection, it is not as reliable. So for the life of me I don't know why the box labels them that way.

I considered (briefly) going back to the owner and asking for an additional $1,600, the going price of fourteen more "squares" of shingles at that time. However, since the owner did not help me with the bid, the fault was mine and mine alone.

Suffice it to say, I have never repeated that mistake.

Chapter 10
I Want *That* Kitchen

Oftentimes, when I meet potential customers to find out what kind of project they want and how much it will cost, the customer has a picture from a magazine of what they want their project to look like when it's finished.

Invariably, the pictures I'm shown are of elaborate bathrooms or kitchens. These pictures or photographs serve many purposes. They give you a feel for the customer's taste, and the budget their project may fit into.

For instance, the customer may show me a picture of a kitchen with maple cabinets, hardwood floors, high-end appliances like a sub-zero refrigerator, and granite tops. If the customer in fact wanted all these choices, you would know that the pricing on this particular kitchen would be fairly expensive.

Or, the customer may be looking for a particular cabinet door style, stain color, or a particular granite edge. In these cases, the picture truly helps both parties in terms of pricing and clarification of styles and colors.

Where these pictures do not help, however, relates to the size of the rooms in these photographs. I have seen bathrooms in the pictures that are at least twenty by fifteen feet wide, which is the size of a small master bedroom. Kitchens are even worse. Some appear to scale out at over thirty feet by thirty feet, enough space for a studio apartment. This does not even take height into account. Whereas the average ceiling height is about eight feet, these kitchens show nine- or ten-foot ceilings creating what I call a dramatic illusion!

For perspective, many guest bathrooms I see are averaging five by ten feet and a modest kitchen averages about fifteen by fifteen feet; although we have remodeled much larger ones. So when a customer says, "I want this kitchen," they seem insulted or puzzled when I tell them they can't have it. Oh sure, I can give them all the components in the picture. I just can't give them the extra space they desire. Not to worry...we can still give them a nice kitchen.

Chapter 11
Jesse

Although I have never been fond of crawling into crawlspaces and under sub floors of potential customers' homes, I find it is a necessity when determining costs on certain types of projects. Needless to say, I have belly crawled beneath my share of homes and none of these trips have been pleasant. I'm not claustrophobic by nature, but one particular job did make me reevaluate my thinking.

The owners of this house showed me an area of their oak floor that appeared to be buckling and they wanted me to see if I could find the cause of this defect. Since there was no evident water source on the floor, I decided to crawl under the floor to look for signs of moisture or dry rot.

It was a cold winter day a few years ago. I brought my little pinscher dog Jesse with me. She is a twenty-eight-pound version of a large Doberman, very intelligent and obedient to a fault. I pulled the cover off the crawl space on the outside of the house. I told Jesse to stay as I pulled on my coveralls. Then grabbing my moisture meter and putting it in my back pocket I took the flashlight and proceeded to worm my way into the small hole, head first, on my belly. I turned on the flashlight to look into the gloom.

Cobwebs hung from the joists and girders overhead; I knocked some of them out of the way with my flashlight. This crawl space was extremely tight, possibly fourteen to fifteen inches from the dirt floor to the bottom of the joists.

The dirt on the ground was extremely dry and fine like baby powder and the slightest movement caused it to swirl. This in turn gave me coughing fits. I was sorry I did not put on a mask, but I did not want to crawl back for it.

I shined the flashlight again to the east end of the building, barely seeing my destination through the dust. It was the brick foundation of a fireplace that protruded above into the family room. The sight depressed me. It had taken a lot of energy just to pull myself through this sea of dust ten feet and it looked to be about fifty more feet to the fireplace.

The only way to progress forward in such a tight place was by using my elbows to pull myself forward in the dirt and then trying to dig my feet in behind me in a pathetic version of a frog kick. I continued in this manner for ten minutes or more—periodically resting, coughing, or trying to spit up the fine dust that was coating the roof of my mouth.

Every few feet or so I had to lower myself even further to avoid dangling wires. The worst area was when I came upon heating ducts and had to flatten myself just to clear them. In these moments I learned what claustrophobia was.

Sometimes crawl spaces have other common attractions to keep the horror story part of my mind occupied; like black widow spiders, rats, or simply a sopping wet sub floor where the mud oozes all over you and cakes up before you exit the crawl space. Any of these would have been preferable to this tight dust bowl.

If I lowered my head to rest I would be lying in cool dust up to my nose. If I raised my head too far, I would hit it on a wood joist. More than once I thought of quitting. The space became even more confining and my mind was focused on trying to force me outside with thoughts of skeletons baked in the desert, death permanently marked in a crawling position.

I decided since I had come this far that I would have to finish the job. I broke out in a cold sweat as I made my way slowly along, the dust now finding additional purchase on my wet face. Finally, I reached the base of the fireplace and took a much-needed rest. I twisted my torso as much as I could in order to reach my moisture meter. After looking around the fireplace and finding no water source, I twisted around onto my back and shined the light on the joists and the underside of the sub floor. All the wood appeared dry. I stuck the prongs of the meter in the wood and it tested dry. No moisture, mission completed.

I worked myself around onto my stomach again, my shoulders finding resistance against the joists. Then I worked my body around until I was facing the direction I started. I was exhausted and sat there for a minute bracing myself for the crawl back.

Suddenly, something touched my face. It was wet and felt large. I let out an involuntary shout and simultaneously jerked my head up striking it hard on the two-by-six joist and drawing blood. As much as this hurt I was more concerned with what was in this dungeon with me. I flashed the light in an arc and suddenly there was Jesse! She had walked her way all the way back and was tall enough that she had to duck to get under some of the HVAC ducting. What a relief! "Good girl, Jesse!"

Later in the day as I reported my findings to the owners and the fact that no water appeared to be causing the floor damage, we hypothesized on any other reasons for the damage. Ironically, it may have been their old dog that precipitated the problem, with an unfortunate accident.

Chapter 12
Who the Hell Are You?

During the course of construction, some customers ask us if we can install a safe in their home. We have installed wall safes, floor safes, and have even built large cabinets around massive safes to conceal them.

In our last home my wife and I decided that it would be nice to have a safe, so one night I pulled the carpet up from under the desk in our office and proceeded to start chopping the concrete on the floor about ten inches away from the outside wall. Our goal was to install a square floor safe, approximately twelve inches square and twelve inches tall.

The first night I used a little electric chipping gun to break the surface. Concrete slabs on residential homes rarely exceeded four inches in thickness so I figured I could chop out the hole with a four-pound sledge hammer and a cold chisel. The chipping seemed to go smoothly even though I didn't have much headroom. I had to sit down under my desk and situate myself over the intended safe hole to do the chipping. There was not much room to control the chipping gun so I was happy when this phase ended.

The next night was when the real problem began. As I sat on my butt and leaned over trying to create leverage with the sledge, I realized I was down about six inches and still all I saw was concrete. This went on for two nights.

Eventually I found out the slab was ten inches thick on this side of the house. Later, as we put our paltry possessions in the safe, I promised myself I would never put in another floor safe.

When we moved several years later, the idea of buying a safe came up again. This time I went to a locksmith who sold safes.

"I need a medium-size safe to put in my home."

"What about that one?" the man says, pointing to a small safe, approximately sixteen inches square.

"This one?" I say pointing as I walk up to it.

"Yup," he says as I bend down to pick it up in my hands and stand up.

"What the heck am I gonna do with this? I can carry it right out of here by myself."

"Who the hell are you?"

"What do you mean?" I say slightly offended.

"I mean who the hell do you think you are? What the hell do you have?"

Now I'm thinking, this guy really knows how to make a sale.

"What are you talking about?"

"Look, someone breaks into your house, they're in there for four to six minutes tops. First they have to find the safe, usually they just pick these houses at random. So, unless you're Tom Cruise they're not looking for your stash of gold coins."

This wise guy has a point. "Four minutes, huh? I'll take it." Who am I to argue with authority?

Chapter 13
Q & A with a Customer

Going over the initial estimate with these clients, I say, "Do you understand these material allowances?"

Husband: "Yes."

Wife: "Oh, sure."

"Well, let me give you another example just to be sure. If you look under allowances on your proposal you picked a certain Monogram refrigerator costing $3,200. Now since we know the model number it was easy to check the price. So in this case, your allowance will match what we actually charged you for the refrigerator. Are you with me?"

Glazed looks, and "yes" in unison.

"Okay, now look down below in lumber material allowances. At today's prices the cost of the lumber to build your room addition is $4,890. Because the price of lumber is so volatile right now the price may be higher or lower when we start your job in two months. At that time I'll present you with the lumber invoices and we will adjust the allowance accordingly. Make sense?"

Husband: "Sure."

Wife: "Do we both sign here?"

Three and a half months later:

Talking to the same clients, "Here is the invoice for draw #3. Item B shows the difference in the cost of the lumber we bid. As you can see, the price of plywood went through the roof. My supplier is saying they're sending all the plywood to Iraq and China and that's driving the price up. I'm telling him, 'Who cares what the excuse is, the fact is the price is higher!' Anyway, the additional cost for lumber is $2600."

Large "O's" on both mouths, with raised eyebrows.

Wife: "Twenty-six hundred bucks? That's crazy!"

Husband, (shouting): "You've got to be kidding, why should we pay for that?"

"Well, a better question would be, why should we have to pay for it?" I say. "We all had to pay more for our cars this year, not to mention the price of gas and milk. Did you guys pay extra for gas and milk?"

Blank stares, and incredulous looks as the husband writes the check. No eye contact. An awkward moment to say the least. I start to say that the money doesn't go to us, but to the supplier, but then think better of it.

This scenario doesn't happen often, but many people don't take the time to actually read their contracts or understand the terms. (Or newspapers for that matter.) The particular year that lumber went up so high and so fast was unusual but seems to be happening more and more in this changing and complex world we live in ... at the end of the same year, in late winter, there were no complaints by another customer as I gave them a nice credit when the price of plywood dropped dramatically. My reward? Cheesecake and coffee.

Chapter 14
The "Eight-Hour" Work Day

Our crews typically work an eight-hour day that starts at about 7:00 a.m. and ends at 3:30 p.m. with a half-hour lunch and two short breaks. This assumes that our customers will let us in their homes at that hour. Our company uses the Nextel phone system, equipped with long-range walkie-talkies, usually assuring instant communication.

One afternoon at approximately 3:10 p.m., I was driving on a freeway overpass near where we do a lot of our work. I happened to glance at the sparse freeway traffic and noticed one of our small company trucks, which are white with an easily recognized logo.

Because of the type of truck I was able to determine which employee happened to be on the freeway at that time. For purposes of this story, we will call him John Doe. No sooner than I have time to assimilate this information, the walkie-talkie portion of my phone activates in the form of a distinctive beep. It is John Doe. Here is a loose translation of our conversation.

"Hey, Mick, what's happening?"

"Not much, John, what's up?"

"I'm getting ready to roll up my tools, and I want to know where I'm gonna be tomorrow?"

"Go back to the same job and finish the trench, John. Oh, by the way while you're there I want you to cover that wood with a tarp. Drive some three-inch screws down into the pile first. I don't want anyone stealing that lumber. I'll see you there first thing in the morning." I smile knowing I just made him go back to the site he claimed he was still at. Petty? Maybe, but then he'd just lied to me; so we both learned a valuable lesson.

A pause and John comes back hesitantly, "Okay ten-four, Mick ... see you in the morning."

"Take care, John." (He drove back to the project and fixed the tarp.)

Initiative in an employee can be a good thing; but claiming eight hours of pay for seven and a half hours of work is not the kind I like. (I wonder if I should check and see what time John starts in the mornings. Oh well, I hope he doesn't get caught in rush-hour traffic. That would be a shame.)

Chapter 15
That's a Shame

One of the aspects we have never worried about in the past is construction theft. Oh, sure there are clauses built into our proposal to cover us against such losses, but sometimes even if it walks like a duck and talks like a duck, it still may not be a duck.

Recently, within a two-week span, we had lumber stolen on two different jobs. On the first one, a resident's addition, we had some special plywood, twelve-inch-wide siding boards, delivered on a Friday afternoon.

This small pile of lumber was dropped right in the owner's driveway. Monday morning it was gone. Now, if I had time to play detective I would start searching the neighbor's yards in a three-block perimeter because I noticed that this particular siding was used on several houses in the neighborhood.

This siding is not made anymore and we had to have it specially milled at a premium price. Maybe one of the neighbors had some dry rot and also knew the siding was no longer available. Or, maybe some kids used it to build a skateboard ramp.

In any event, the material disappeared and since it wasn't protected or put under lock and key, we felt that this was not the owner's responsibility or fault. The final tally: $700 in the red. I could understand if some kids took the siding, but cannot fathom the gall it would take for an adult to steal it.

The second incident was slightly more painful. On this project we also dropped off a load of lumber, approximately $4,000 worth of plywood and two-by-sixes on a Friday morning. Two of my men set up the project that day and installed a few pieces of lumber, which was the start of a handicap ramp project at a local school.

This time the lumber was dropped inside the school grounds and behind a locked gate. Since it looked like it might rain that weekend we were allowed to store the plywood inside of an adjacent classroom.

When the men returned on Monday, every piece of lumber that wasn't screwed or nailed down was gone, including the plywood that was inside the classroom and the scrap pieces that were cut earlier. We questioned school employees, maintenance men, teachers, and other contractors working another project on site. No one knew a thing.

I felt like Colombo in the ignorant persona he uses during the first half of all his movies.

I called my contact, the man who hired us to do this project. His reply after hearing how, where, when, and what was stolen was, "That's a shame."

The expression on my face: Priceless.

The profit on the project: Price plus less.

The protection our contract afforded us: Useless.

The customer on this job was a repeat customer that we had a long-standing relationship with. Sometimes it just pays to eat the loss and move on. There's always tomorrow.

Chapter 16
Who Peed on My Floor

We were in the midst of building a family room addition for a nice couple in Sacramento in the spring. At the time the new space had a roof and was waterproofed, up to and including wrapping the exterior walls with wood siding. In the interior, sheetrock had just been applied to the walls and we were waiting for a sheetrock nail inspection. The floors were built over a raised foundation and at this stage of the project the floors showing were still the tongue-and-groove plywood. Eventually carpet and pad would go over this sub-floor after texture and painting were complete.

It was a warm Friday afternoon and Joan, the wife, wanted to show me something in the new space. At this stage the new space was separated from the existing kitchen by a temporary plastic wall, which we folded over and walked through.

Joan walked over to the outside wall where sunlight was shining into the room. I smelled a distinct odor as Joan pointed to the floor in the corner. I followed her finger to a wet spot on the floor.

"I think one of your men urinated in our new room."

"WHAT?" (Boy, she doesn't pull any punches.)

"One of your men peed on the floor right there."

"Are you kidding me?"

"No, I'm dead serious."

"You're saying that one of my brothers just decided to pee on the floor, in your house, in broad daylight, even though I have a portable toilet not twenty-five feet away on the side of your house, with a door and privacy?"

"Well, I'm not saying one of your brothers did it. It could have been the dry-wallers." (She actually said this with a straight face.)

As I listened to her I almost laughed out loud. The combination of Joan's southern accent coupled with what she was implying made me think I was in the middle of a skit on *Saturday Night Live*.

I regained my composure and asked, "Why would one of my men do something like this? I have known all these dry-wallers for several years, not to mention the fact that I was raised with my brothers. I know they didn't do it!"

"I just don't know, Mick. How could this have happened?"

Without answering, I dropped down into the pushup position and got my nose as close as I dared to the wet spot, then immediately pushed myself back up.

"Joan, I hate to tell you this, but this is cat urine."

"Are you sure?"

"I know cat urine when I smell it. Would you like to smell it yourself?"

"No, that's quite all right."

"Joan, lots of times on these remodels, people's pets, especially cats, tend to get upset and create mischief; like tearing up a couch with their claws, spraying the furniture, or peeing on the floor."

We both laughed.

"I can't believe it. I feel so foolish. I hope you'll accept my apology. I didn't mean to offend you."

"No offense taken."

A thought popped into my head as I drove away. Human nature ... sometimes it's just our nature to cast blame on the obvious.

Chapter 17
False Alarm

Years ago we were working on an isolated home overlooking the Sacramento River. We had worked on this particular home several times. The owner wasn't going to be home, but earlier he had given me the key and his alarm code.

My coworker and I pulled our toolboxes out of the truck and attached our tool belts to our waists. I walked up to the front door, used the key to open it and made my way through the entry to the keypad on the wall in the adjacent hall.

I punched in the numbers and pressed "Enter" and then called to Roger to bring in the tarps. Less than a minute later the house alarm started blaring at an extremely loud and obnoxious frequency. The sound was deafening.

I looked around on the keypad for an alarm company phone number. When that didn't work I went down the hall into the closet and found the control panel. Short of breaking the unit I could find no way to stop the screeching sirens. We finally exited the house unable to endure the noise.

I pulled out my cell phone to call the owner, but I couldn't get a signal. There was nothing left to do now but wait ... and wait. A sheriff's car finally pulled up twenty-five minutes after the alarm went off. By this time we were not in the best of moods, since we were already wasting daylight.

Two officers got out of the police car and sauntered up to where we were leaning on my pickup.

"What's happening out here?" the lead officer asks.

"Not much … we were getting ready to build some cabinets. The alarm code the owner gave us didn't work."

"It was bogus, man!" Roger chirps in.

I give Roger a look, but the officer dismissed him with a turn of the head.

The sheriff nods to his partner, who apparently calls in and somehow connects with the alarm company to cancel the false alarm. He makes some more small talk and then they take off, heading to the next crisis.

I sit there happy, but perplexed. Happy because we weren't hassled, perplexed because the sheriffs didn't check our I.D.'s, or even ask us our names, not to mention the twenty-five-minute delay getting there. More than enough time to ransack a home.

Apparently, a couple of slick crooks can walk around wearing tool belts and carrying a Skilsaw ostensibly to perform carpentry tasks, all the while adding excess weight to their pickup trucks in the form of TV's, VCR's, and assorted jewelry. (Not a very comforting thought.)

As for the paranoid owner, I'll have to touch bases on his penchant for constantly changing his code.

Chapter 18
"I'm Taking the Discount"

A customer recently ran me through a series of hoops. Although I know that he is an attorney, he could have made a decent living with Barnum & Bailey. In his defense, I should have known better. His architectural plans were weak on details and had many suspect measurements, which made this job difficult to begin with. So to help move the job along and keeping it from falling hopelessly behind schedule, we began performing some changes and additional work prior to obtaining a signed change order from the owners.

Initially there was no sign there would be any problem. The owner paid the first two draws called out in the contract in full and on time. However, when I finally made out the change order for electrical changes we already completed, the owner said he wanted more details and breakdowns.

"What kind of details do you need? You and your wife were the ones that directed my electrician to make these changes. The hours for each task are listed. It's all there in black and white. We didn't even charge you for all the additional time wasted in the field and in the office."

"I just need more of it broken down, Mick, and material receipts. That's all I ask."

That was spoken very calmly; polished. I almost applauded. Rather than argue, I agreed I would try to get more detail for him and then I would expect payment.

Two days later, after getting some more information from the electrician, I re-faxed the invoice with the new information. I also stated that he could take a $250 discount in the spirit of compromise.

Approximately one month later after many more faxes and change orders, more accounting and more ultimatums, the owner paid the change order. The only problem was the amount due was $2,400, and he paid approximately $1,300. At the bottom of his accounting he had also taken a $250 discount.

I almost laughed out loud when I read this. I called him and told him how sorry I was but we aren't in the habit of rewarding our customers for not paying their bills. He eventually wrote us a check for $250 and signed the change order, although he wrote the price as TBD (to be determined). As of press time we are still waiting for the past-due balance.

You see, in our line of work, the words "change order" have become synonymous with a dirty word, and often change orders are not good for the owner or the contractor since they usually cost the customer more money and can cost the contractor time and profits. They can, however, be beneficial in many instances such as changes in paint colors, changing wall locations listed in the plans, crediting the owner for deleting an item such as a refrigerator, or for any item that changes the original contract price. Above all, they are actually a record of changes that may occur during the course of what may be a six-month job. The change order can serve as a document used to avoid disputes after the project is complete. It helps both parties remember what was changed, and why.

The more complete a set of plans are and the more prepared the owner and contractor are, the less chance there is for an abundance of changes. Of course you will always run into the customers that can't make up their minds and are constantly influenced by outside sources. These are the customers I wish I could anticipate before we enter into a business relationship.

The moral of the story: Get those change orders signed. Before the work gets done!

Chapter 19
"The Check's in the Mail"

This story can also fall under the heading "Disorganized Office" or "We're Not the Bank of America." The latter title refers to a growing trend where the customer treats contractual invoices/draws as if they were a mortgage payment or an electric bill. In other words, they pay the bill in thirty days or more, or it gets buried in the stack of bills on the counter. Some of the construction payments or draws can go as high as $30,000 for a progress payment and the contract verbiage usually says these payments are due as soon as specific part of the work is complete.

For example, draw #3 will be due ($22,000) when all drywall is installed. In our business cash flow is important, especially when it comes to keeping a job running on schedule.

This story however, unfortunately falls under the formal heading of "Disorganized Office." While working on a large kitchen remodel project for a repeat customer, we simultaneously took on a smaller project for a neighbor that lived in an adjacent condominium. The gentleman in question was older, gruff, and (to be polite) "quite particular" so we were happy when his job was complete.

Since the size of this job was under $3,000, we only required one payment—which was due at the completion of the project. Three weeks passed with no check, then four, and finally in the fifth week we decided to act.

After re-billing the customer, I waited a few days and then gave him a call. I figured as particular as this man was, he wouldn't mind if I was a little particular about receiving payment.

"Mr. Johnson?"

"Yeah, who's this?"

"It's Mick Profacci. How are you?"

"What do you want?" (So much for small talk.)

"I'm calling about the payment that's due for the work we did for you. Are you satisfied with the work?"

"I paid you, a long time ago."

"There's no record of your payment, Mr. Johnson. We sure can use a check. If you did send a check, you could stop payment on it and send us another one. We'll even pay the bank charge."

"Dadgum it!"

Eventually Mr. Johnson wrote another check. Two months later I was looking down into my file cabinet when something caught my eye. I squeezed two fingers between the files and back of the drawer and pulled out a little rectangular piece of paper. Mr. Johnson's original check.

After much consternation, I called him and apologized.

Chapter 20
Smoke Break

In the early days when the concept of becoming a general contractor was not yet fully formed in my mind, I was busy framing homes with a friend who eventually taught me much about the carpentry trade: how to frame walls, build roof structures, and the like.

It was summertime and we were framing large apartment buildings. At the time, we had finished framing the walls on the first floor, rolled the joists which would support the second floor, and were now applying the tongue-and-groove plywood sheeting, which would eventually become the flooring for the second floor.

Three of us were working on this floor—Mark, myself, and Dale. Dale was fairly new to the crew and we were still getting used to each other's nuances and idiosyncrasies. One of these peculiarities belonged to Dale.

Dale smoked cigarettes and would occasionally stop what he was doing to light up and smoke one. This was slightly irritating because as a non-smoker I assumed that maybe Dale could smoke and work at the same time; a novel concept. Or maybe he would smoke during lunch or during the two breaks we took each day.

While this was a source of continued puzzlement, what happened next really aroused our curiosity. Dale had just finished smoking a cigarette. A few minutes later he drops his tool bag on the plywood deck, climbs down the ladder, and walked approximately one hundred feet to a portable toilet onsite.

Judging from the duration of the time spent in this little suffocating, odorous, four-by-four-foot box, we assumed that Dale was taking care of the type of business that required sitting down. A few minutes later Dale strolled back up to the deck with a satisfied look on his face and proceeded to strap on his tool belt and go back to work.

Perplexed, I said, "Dale, I have a great idea. Next time you head over to the porta-potty, bring your smokes with you. This way you can kill three birds with one stone."

"How's that?"

"Well, when you get in there, besides relieving yourself, you can take a smoke break at the same time. Then as an added benefit, the cigarette smoke will kill any offensive odors in there."

The perplexed look I had passed over to Dale's face, while Mark stood grinning from ear to ear, all the while working with a cigarette dangling from his mouth!

Chapter 21
If You Eliminate the Obvious …

I try to help past customers whenever I can. The following customers are no exception. We had completed several projects in this home within the past ten years—extending the dining room, adding some beautiful bay windows in the kitchen, and remodeling two bathrooms. Jerry and Barbara liked our work and we in turn enjoyed working for them. It is just this type of relationship that you strive for in this business, and one our company does not take for granted.

Jerry called me one morning, explaining that there was a strange odor emanating from the area of their foyer. Barbara had already called a heating and air subcontractor and that company had come out, checked over the HVAC system, and told her the odor was not the ducts or furnace and they had no idea what it was or where it was coming from. Jerry was apologetic about calling me, but asked if I would come and take a look.

When I arrived at Jerry's home, I smelled an unpleasant musty odor as soon as I walked in the front door. Jerry again apologized for wasting my time but said he thought if anyone could find the problem, I could.

The first thing I noticed was that the odor was strongest in the foyer, an area about eight feet by eight feet. Upon questioning, Jerry clarified that the smell was constant but only occurred in the foyer.

I started by looking for anything obvious. I located a doorbell transformer in a closet adjacent to the foyer. Climbing up a ladder, I put my nose close to it and sniffed, thinking maybe this electrical unit was causing the smell, but it wasn't.

Next I checked the air-conditioning vent on a wall right off the foyer. I knew it had already been checked by the HVAC company, but I wanted to eliminate all the obvious possibilities. The ducts smelled clean.

I asked Jerry more questions. Did they have a cat? No. Any other pets? No. Had the door been left open so a wild animal might have come and gone? (That got a strange look!) No; no animals at all had been in the house.

Once the ceiling and walls were cleared, I looked at the floor.

The entry/foyer floor consisted of twelve-by-twelve-inch marble tiles. The living room, directly adjacent to the foyer was covered in plush carpet. I bent down, got on my knees, and started smelling the carpet, especially at the corners where the carpet met the walls. I was now searching for any sign of mold or mildew, which can take many forms. I pulled a moisture detector out of my back pocket and stuck the prongs in the base trim below the carpet line. There was no sign of moisture.

I asked Jerry if they had hired any new cleaners lately or if they had used any special cleaning solutions on the furniture—or anywhere else for that matter. To the best of his knowledge, he didn't think so.

As I stood up and looked around, I realized that I was running out of ideas. It was looking like I wasn't going to pull a rabbit out of my hat this time. I walked back into the foyer area, staring toward the front door. Could it be the door? I leaned closer. No, that wasn't it.

But the odor was definitely strongest right in front of the door. It was a musty unpleasant odor; one I couldn't readily match to any odors I had smelled in the past. I was now standing on a beautiful round Persian-style rug, about four feet in diameter, centered on the foyer tiles.

It occurred to me that I usually enjoyed this kind of challenge; and it was always satisfying to find a solution. These challenges were mostly along the lines of a leak and involved finding where water was entering a house. In the past, smells and odors had been clues to solutions, not puzzles in themselves.

As I finished that thought, I bent down lower to admire the beautiful rug, running my fingers through its luxurious threading. I wondered why I hadn't remembered it from previous visits. It was very striking! I asked Jerry how long they'd had the rug and he said Barbara bought it a few months ago at an antique mall.

I raised my fingers under my nose. Sure enough, the odor was pungent on my fingers. As I lifted the rug up, the source of the musty smell became obvious to Jerry also.

"Well, Jerry, it's hard to believe that so much odor could come from such a small rug." We had a good laugh over this and I left with Jerry promising to tell me if they were ever able to get the smell removed from the rug.

I thought about it as I drove away. It seems to me that the combination of being on non-absorbent marble, in a confined area, and with limited air movement because no air ducts pointed directly at it; allowed the odor from the rug to hover in a low noxious cloud which was stirred up every time someone walked through the front door. Each person's passage would pull that cloud along and up so that the "bad smell" was only noticed when it finally rose to nose level—a ways away from the actual culprit.

I didn't get any new work that day and I saw no need to charge such good customers for this service call. I am glad I found the source of the problem and even happier for the good will it created.

Chapter 22
An Act of God

An act of God is a term often seen in contracts, especially in remodel contracts where inclement weather can often dictate the length of a project. The clause protects the contractor against delays which are out of their control. I have seen many kinds of weather slow down or stop a job, from pouring rain, to snow and icicles. I have had to cover concrete in one rare instance to keep it from freezing, in California of all places. I have even seen a customer's entire collection of grandfather clocks stop due to the shaking caused by an earthquake. It also created waves in a pool, although it did not stop the job.

Once in the foothills near Folsom, California, we had to contend with rattlesnakes while working under the crawlspaces of some homes under construction. Most of these instances were surprising, but not shocking. That is until one memorable spring day in April when two of my brothers were forced off their work site. No, it didn't rain. It wasn't too hot either. There wasn't even a big Doberman guarding the backyard; and it wasn't a wayward blue jay that flew through an open window. What happened on that spring day started with an imperceptible hum. When it rapidly grew to a loud hum, my brothers looked up from the foundation to see a giant swarm of bees. Too stunned to move, they watched as what looked like thousands of bees formed a mass about the size of a football around an electrical mast six feet over their heads.

Both men slowly backed up, not taking their eyes off the bees and trying not to create any motion that would antagonize them.

The owners eventually called a beekeeper that relocated the bees, but on that beautiful seventy-five-degree day with a slight breeze, no one worked on that part of the project for three hours.

Chapter 23
Hothouse or Outhouse

Portable toilets, the colorful little outhouses often seen in front of construction sites, seem to bring the worst out in some people. This includes a variety of frustrated poets, if the prose I've seen is any indication. Portable toilets are also a necessity. They are the source of much mischief, paranoia, anxiety, and can literally be a life-saving device. They are incongruous and ubiquitous. Anyone who has ever used one knows of what I speak.

While these tiny houses have been occupied, I have seen firecrackers thrown in them. I have seen boards nailed across the door to block the user's escape. (This usually only works with the wood variety, which is popular in blue in these parts, versus the lime-green more modern plastic version.) I have seen trucks pushed up against them to trap someone. I have witnessed forklifts lifting up porta-potties to create a new element of horror for the user; and unfortunately I have seen them tipped over while the receptacle was occupied. Horror of horrors! I have seen these units so full, it is hard to believe a human being actually walked in and used it. And finally I knew someone who dropped their keys in one, and I don't mean on the floor. Dropping the keys was unfortunate. Searching for them was along the lines of idiotic.

On the other hand, *vacant* outhouses usually bring out the bolder morons and cretins. One morning we found the remains of a porta-potty that had been incinerated. The only evidence of its existence was a puddle of blue liquid and a slimy green trail melted on top of the asphalt. Another night a wooden one was burned to the ground, which also burned the public restroom next to it, costing the city thousands of dollars to repair.

Another odd thing: One morning Gary, a city employee and the man who hired us for this city park project, opened the door of the double-wide porta-potty, a unit built to accommodate handicapped persons, and said, "Mick, I want to show you something." I stuck my head in the door and saw a huge pile of human feces on top of the closed toilet seat. I burst out laughing until I heard what Gary said next: "You guys are going to have to clean that up."

"Sorry, Gary," I replied, "that's not part of our job description."

Gary eventually relented. The rest of my day passed by quickly in part because I couldn't help visualizing what the fool looked like as he left his gift to the city.

Chapter 24
Tower of Power

I always tell my customers to set a budget for their remodel and then stick to that budget. If they don't, it's very easy to get carried away and find yourself thousands of dollars over the original remodel cost in their contract.

How? Lots of ways.

For example, I can't remember a customer ever telling me, "Hey, Mick, we don't need granite on our kitchen countertops after all. Just put some Formica on the counters." More than likely it's the other way around.

Or the customer starts shopping for appliances. Their budget calls for a $500 allowance for a dishwasher—determined during my initial meeting with the customer. Since they had not already picked a specific dishwasher at the time we met, I had asked what type and quality dishwasher they wanted. They told me something similar to the existing would do just fine—which would cost under $500 to replace.

Later, when they started shopping they found they could purchase a dishwasher with stainless steel insides, superior cleaning power, and total quiet while the machine ran. Naturally the owner chose one of these models, at a cost of twelve hundred dollars. So you see how easy it is to upgrade.

I tried a different tack with some other new customers. The day before I was going to sit down in my office with this couple and sign a remodel contract (in excess of $300,000), Sally called and told me she wanted to make a change in the powder room.

The next day, after we reviewed the documents, the owners signed the proposal and asked if there was anything else. I pulled out a change order with the powder room change she requested to make the vanity top limestone instead of tile. The cost listed on the change order was $240. On the bottom in large block letters I had written NO CHARGE.

Dave and Sally both saw it at the same time. "That's very nice of you." Dave said.

I answered in a mock-stern voice, "Well, I want you to put this on your refrigerator to remind you that changes are our enemy."

They both laughed, but took what I said to heart. Ironically, *their* change was requested with plenty of advance notice and the only cost associated with it was the raise in material pricing. Many others cause more trouble.

Now, after seeing this same pattern over many years, and constantly warning my customers of these dangers, I felt that I personally was immune to this disease. Just as many humans are pack rats, (I speak from experience, having seen hundreds of customers' garages, closets, and spare bedrooms), people in this "me, me, me" society also can't seem to help themselves from feeling that they need something better, bigger, faster, harder, or covered in stainless steel.

Case in point, when my wife and I finally got around to remodeling our own master bath we, like my customers, had many choices to make. One of those choices was the style of showerhead and mixer valve. Many of my customers had also been using a second showerhead on a sliding arm with an extension hose to wash their hair and clean the shower. We thought this was a great idea, so I started looking through catalogues.

In one such catalogue there was a section with shower towers. These towers had many expensive extras, like dual showerheads on adjustable telescopic poles (my favorite feature), four pulsing jets that slide up and down and spray directly at you, a hand-held showerhead, and the ability to use any combination of these you desired. All wrapped in a beautiful brushed nickel finish.

I have installed two or three towers over the years. The last one was about four and one-half feet tall and in my recollection cost close to $1,000. The particular one we were looking at was over six feet tall and almost a foot wide and was very impressive in all its modernistic glory. I have seen it in the catalogues for years, but none of my customers ever purchased one.

My wife loved the unit and we ordered it. My salesperson called and asked if I knew how much this unit cost. I told her I had an idea. To make a long story short, my idea was totally off base. The tower cost in excess of $3,000, the price of a used Volkswagen in some places.

Since we were already emotionally committed and because my wife absolutely loved it, we went ahead and purchased our shower tower. We rationalized that house prices were skyrocketing and we had no plans to move—which lessened the pain somewhat. A year has passed and we both still love the tower for its functionality and for the privilege of having our own personal showerhead customized for our individual heights. What did our material budget start out with for a nice showerhead, mixer valve handles, and a slide arm with a handle-held sprayer? Five hundred and fifty dollars. Enough said.

Chapter 25
Where's the Time Clock?

The receptionist who had been with our company for over ten years recently retired. She is a very lovely lady and often made me feel like my mom was still alive. We played practical jokes on each other all the time.

Once I inserted a line of verbiage in a proposal that said, "The British invented the game of golf and the Americans perfected it." I figured this would rile her good since she is Welsh and proud of it. Not to mention the fact that she and her husband watch golf on television all the time. The first time I knew I could get to her was during one of the Ryder Cups. Colin Montgomerie was playing poorly and I let Maggie know by way of pronouncing Colin's name wrong. I still haven't heard the last of that mistake.

When she put the proposal on my desk it was all typed including the rogue phrase. I guess she didn't read my bids.

On my birthday she would invariably send a card with a toilet as the main theme. Where she found these, I'll never know. But I always enjoyed them.

About three years ago, I walked into the reception area at around 9:15 in the morning. Maggie had just walked in the office and set her purse on the desk.

"What the heck are you doing here so early, Maggie?"

"Why 'wotever' do you mean, Mick?"

"Well, you don't start until 9:30 and it's only 9:15."

Maggie leaned over and punched me in the arm while simultaneously saying, "Well you're going to get yours Mick, you know I start at 9:00!"

"I'm not kidding, I thought you started at 9:30!"

"Oh, Mick."

(I meant it. I really had thought she started at 9:30!)

Chapter 26
The Joke's on You

My brother Tony has a very dry sense of humor. If you were not paying close attention you may miss it entirely; which brings me to the Pearce project.

Tony was running this job, a second-story master bedroom extension and a remodel of the adjoining master bath including the addition of an elaborate skylight cut into an existing concrete tile roof. The pitch of the roof was very steep, which created a very tall light well that started from the ceiling and went up eight feet above. My brother also "flared" the light well as it met the ceiling, creating a dramatic look and causing more light to diffuse into the room.

In addition, the skylight had remote shutters, remote control with electric motors to open and close the skylight, and a rain sensor, which would automatically close the skylight when it started raining.

The Pearces were the type of couple that asked a lot of questions, many of them technical. My brothers, Tony and Tom, were happy to explain things to them. Tony had just finished installing the skylight over a special wood curb built on the roof, which had been flashed with a lead material so it could be molded around the curved concrete tiling on the roof surface. This in turn formed a shield or diverter, which prevented water from leaking into the house around the skylight.

Mr. Pearce, arm around his wife, looked up at the skylight and asked, "This is pretty amazing, Tony. Have you done many skylights like this before?"

Without missing a beat, and totally deadpan, Tony states, "No. This is our first one."

Tom adds, "Mick said we have to learn how to do these sooner or later."

The couple, silent for a few beats, looked at each other, and not entirely convinced, both laughed uncertainly and walked out of the bathroom.

Tom related the conversation to me at the end of the day as they packed up their tools.

"You've got to be kidding me, Tony. That's not the kind of seed we want planted in our customer's heads!"

"Don't worry, Mick. I'm pretty sure they knew we were joking."

Two days later it started raining hard. The guys had just shown up at the job. As they carried their tools in through the garage, Mr. Pearce came through the garage door, frantic. "The skylight's leaking, Tony! Some of the drywall's wet."

"What are we gonna do, honey?" his wife asked, appearing behind him.

The contingent all climbed the stairs wordlessly, Tony in the lead. He walked into the bath and looked up at the skylight, rain pattering hard on the acrylic surface, but no apparent signs of a leak. Color slowly returned to Tony's face as Mr. Pearce yelled, "Touché!" and they all laughed heartily, each for a different reason.

Chapter 27
Here Today Gone Tomorrow

Sometimes you just can't move fast enough to please someone. I agreed to squeeze a customer's bathroom extension into our schedule within the next few months. She was a good customer and the job was in the neighborhood where we were working on several other projects.

A month after we had our last conversation, Karen called and asked why she kept seeing these other projects moving forward, and her job had not even been started. Karen was very anxious and I told her again that we were getting close to starting.

A week later Karen called and insisted that I stop stalling and to get her job started immediately. Wishing to avoid any undue conflict, I enlisted the help of my father and pulled three men off another project. (So much for "squeezing" her on the schedule.)

The men broke ground the next morning and with the skilled direction of my father, they had the foundation dug, graded, and formed, all ready for the first inspection in just two days.

A little background would be helpful here. My father, sixty-six years old at the time, still seemed to outwork all of us. He instilled his work ethic and moral code in all of us. Most everything we know in the construction trade we learned from him and we were happy to have him on our projects.

I had an inspection called the next day to inspect the footings. Once this passed we would be ready to pour the concrete footings, which would eventually support the house walls. Fortunately we did not have to run the new sewer line for the bath toilets, sinks, or shower yet because we were building the house on a raised floor with a crawl space, allowing the plumber to work on the sewer pipe later in the schedule.

The afternoon after I met the inspector, Karen called me.

"Mick, I need you to stop working on the bathroom."

Silence… "What?"

"You have to stop working on the bath. I just bought a new house down the street and it's going to need some remodel work inside. Can you come and look at it with me?"

"What about this place? The landscaping's all torn out, the footings are all dug, and we're ready to pour concrete."

"Just take everything out. We're going to move into this other one."

"Holy cow, you're not joking!"

As I mentioned earlier, Karen is a good customer. She pays her bills, has a great sense of style and space, and she gives us a lot of work. After talking to several of my men, I met them at the project at dusk and proceeded to tear down all of our work, filled the trenches, re-graded the dirt, and hauled off all the material and equipment. (I spared my father this embarrassment.)

We completed this work in darkness, not from any sense of guilt, but from the realization that in a neighborhood where we had high exposure and many customers, I couldn't help thinking that the first thought that would come to most peoples minds was that our company had made some kind of monumental mistake.

Karen paid her bill on time. Three weeks later we started tearing off drywall in her new bathroom.

Chapter 28
Speech Impediment

I was winding up a particularly long day last winter. It had started in pre-dawn pitch-blackness and threatened to end after dark. I had set up an appointment to give a bid to a repeat customer at 4:30 that afternoon not knowing that I was going to feel physically and mentally exhausted.

At approximately 4:15 I stopped at a local coffee shop and quickly drank a large French roast cup of coffee, something I rarely do at that time of the day. If I do drink coffee that late, it tends to keep me awake.

As I knocked on the Hogans' door, I felt refreshed, almost giddy. We greeted each other and then proceeded to sit down around the bar in their kitchen—one that our company had remodeled several months earlier. I asked some questions about the new remodel and took some notes. It seemed suddenly quiet. I looked up from my notes and both Mr. and Mrs. Hogan were staring at me. Puzzled, I stared back.

Mr. Hogan broke the silence.

"Mick, is something wrong?"

"What do you mean, Stan?"

"Well, I feel that we know you pretty well after our last remodel, wouldn't you say?"

"Sure, I feel like we've become friends."

"That's true. The reason I ask, Mick, is you normally talk fast and I know that's typical with most of you New Yorkers; but today you are talking extremely fast. (pause) Are you on drugs?"

"What? Well that's a first. I don't think I have ever been asked that question during a bid." Nervous laughter from the three of us, then I continued. "Guys, I've been up since three o'clock this morning. My face feels like a mask that is about to crack. On the way over I stopped to get a large cup of coffee at Mocha Joe's. I guess I should have gotten the small size."

We all had a good laugh.

Looking back, I'm glad I was with a couple I knew. I probably would not have received a callback if I'd been at a stranger's house, and if I did they might have called to say "Sorry" with no explanation. Their dinner conversation that night would have included an interesting discussion on "that whacked-out dope-head contractor."

Chapter 29
No, It Hurts over There

One of my brothers was doing a job at a customer's home. The scope of the work consisted of removing and replacing the front entry door, jamb, and trim and installing the door the customers chose. The total cost of the project was about $800.

Prior to starting the project, my brother and I both noticed many scratches in the entry oak floor. This floor was approximately five feet wide by approximately ten feet long. The floor as well worn, and my best guess was it had never been refinished in the twenty-five-plus years since the house was built. I told Ralph to be careful anyway and to cover the floor with a tarp.

The special order door was delivered and Ralph proceeded to remove the old unit and fit in the new one. The door fit in the opening nicely and the trim was all mitred cleanly. All in all, everything went well for such a small project.

After looking at the work I sent the customer an invoice. Instead of receiving a check, I received a letter from the husband, who happened to be an attorney. Summarizing, he stated that he and his wife noticed that scratches were made on their oak entry floor, and they would need the entire floor refinished or replaced.

I called the customer and told him I received his letter and I would check with my brother regarding the nature of these scratches. I beeped up Ralph and asked if he scratched the floor. "No way," he said. "I only used a few hand tools and I set them on a towel."

"Did you cover the rest of the floor with a tarp?"

"No I didn't, but I didn't scratch that floor, Mick."

After this conversation I contemplated for a while. It was obvious the floor was in terrible shape prior to our arrival and even more obvious that the owners must have known themselves. The problem, looking back, is that we made three mistakes.

The first was not taking pictures of the floor, and/or notifying the customer in writing as to the condition of the floor. The second mistake was not covering the entire work area. As I told my brother later, if he had tarped off the area, there would have been less chance of being blamed for scratches or any damage, no matter how sincere a customer may be.

The third mistake was all mine. We had already performed another small project in this owner's dining room, removing a wall and adding a beam. During that project I walked into the room where the work was going on, but my brothers were not there.

I heard voices in another part of the house and found my brothers in a room adjacent to the remodeled area, and across the hall.

"What are you guys doing here?" I asked, as if I couldn't figure out why they had taping knives and joint compound in their hands.

"The customer told us you said it was okay to fix these cracks. She said they weren't here before we started construction."

Before I continue, I will say that the settling cracks the guys were repairing probably cost our company about ninety dollars and our firm did absorb the cost. The problem here is also a layered one and measures have since been taken to avoid this type of situation again.

If a customer asks the men onsite to perform additional work, they have to sign a change order first so they will acknowledge their request for additional work along with additional cost if any.

Peeling the second layer of this problem is a phenomenon I believe I have identified early in my career. What I have found is that people have a tendency to assume that anything that goes wrong in the house while the construction guys are there must have been caused by the construction guys.

We have all been guilty of this from time to time. I have been guilty of it with regards to my truck engine and my ignorance of its workings. Still, it doesn't make it any easier and, in the case of these customers, even less so.

You see, the areas where my brothers were repairing cracks were across a hall and in another room. I'm not an engineer, but I can say with some certainty that one has nothing to do with the other, especially after looking closely at the cracks, which were by no means fresh.

We decided not to argue over these repairs and just move on, but part of me couldn't let it go. While on the phone with the husband, I asked him what his wife did for a living. He said she was a masseuse. What follows is a paraphrase of that conversation:

"Can I ask you a hypothetical question?"

"Go ahead," he said, the attorney in him unable to resist.

"If I went in to see your wife to massage my shoulder she would charge me a set fee for that wouldn't she?"

"Sure or you would get an hourly rate."

"So if I paid her, say forty dollars for a shoulder massage, and then told her I needed to work on my calf because now it's tight, would she charge me for that?"

"I would say she would have to. It takes more time."

"That's exactly my point."

This customer came to us through a referral and wanted us to do more work. They didn't want any "hard feelings." Actually there weren't any. We gave the customer their entry door, labor with parts for free, and asked them not to call us again. "We simply can't afford to work for you." (Mistake number 3 rectified.)

Chapter 30
Tiny Tidbits

I am a volunteer in the local chapter of the Kiwanis Organization. We were getting ready to move a lot of heavy furniture for a flea market we hold every year to raise money. Some of the guys asked if I had any more strong guys that could help, so I beeped up one of my employees on my Nextel phone.

I arrived before my employee and while we were waiting around one of the members asked how many people I was bringing. I told him just one person and as I looked up he was walking across the street coming towards us.

"Who are you bringing?" Jim asked.

"Tiny."

"Tiny?"

"Yup, that's him," I said as I pointed to Tiny. Tiny is a mountain of a man, weighing approximately 330 pounds. He is solidly built and has to practically duck his head to go through doorways. He is also one of the gentlest people I have ever met.

"That's Tiny?" Jim says in awe and in a quiet whisper.

"He sure is," I said.

"Well, that's Mr. Tiny to you," he says.

When I interview potential employees, at the end of every

interview I usually tell everyone approximately the same two things: Show up to the job on time, and tell me in advance if you can't make it to work. Keep the line of communication open and you won't have any problems with me. If you don't you won't last long here. This was all stated in a manner-of-fact tone.

Tiny came into my office and I took notice of his mass and presence. We were nearing the end of his interview, so I proceeded with my ending "speech."

"Tiny, if you don't mind, could you make sure you show up to work on time?" (Spoken in a singsong voice.)

"Sure, Mick."

"Thanks, Tiny, see you on Monday."

Chapter 31
Dreams

Oh, how my job description has changed over twenty-five years!

I remember a time when a new twenty-four-ounce framing hammer was all I could think of. Better yet, the prospect of getting a brand-new Skil Saw with an extended cord and using my other one for a spare was more than I could hope for. Even a new pickup truck with lumber racks and a theft-proof toolbox in the back was an exciting event.

Working outdoors was something else I enjoyed as a carpenter who framed houses. Framing a house from start to finish was always rewarding. There was a starting and ending point. You could stand back and look at what you had accomplished. You were your own man. If you wanted to take a break at ten o'clock in the morning and eat a large breakfast as you read the sports section, you just did it.

But now, I sit in my new office, looking out a window that does not open, listening for sounds I cannot hear. When we moved into this new office several months ago I'm embarrassed to say that I became extremely excited about the prospect of shopping for a new, functional desk. I spent quite a bit of time choosing a quality chair that would support my back for the many hours I would be using it. I can swivel around and roll on the hard floor and reach my files without getting up. It's the little things in life you look forward to.

Now each day I work off a "to-do" list, hoping to actually finish something. Anything. An exciting moment for me is when the phone doesn't ring for ten minutes. Or when I get two checks in the mail.

I still go out to the job sites, see the guys working and joking around, and wondering where my nail bags are. I've now come full circle. Last year I bought a battery-operated saw, with a drill and a Sawzall, and can't wait to find something to cut in my garage. (My brothers have long since absconded with all my old precious tools.) Then I remember the splinters swelling my fingers, the sawdust sticking to the sweat on my chest and arms, the jolt through my body after getting shocked because the cord to my saw was standing in water, the aching joints, the cold mornings where I couldn't feel the tips of my fingers.

The grass is truly greener on the other side. Always. No matter which side you're on. What? You expected some philosophical ribbon to tie it all together? After all, this is only a dream.

Chapter 32
Liability Insurance, Use It, Lose It?

While I'll be the first to admit that our liability insurance coverage allows me to sleep better at night, sometimes thoughts creep into my dreams on this subject which are more in tune with nightmares. Thoughts like, while in our state it is not required that we carry liability insurance; we would be fools not to carry it.

For a small general contractor the annual cost of a liability policy can reach the high thousands, assuming you have never filed any claims. Unfortunately, the privilege of shelling out all this cash does not guarantee that you will continue to have coverage.

Insurers will drop you for a variety of reasons, the most frustrating of them is for simply being a general contractor. I'm not sure what your chances of keeping your insurance are if you actually file a claim, since we have never used ours in almost seventeen years of doing business. Simply never finding out is privilege enough for me.

Liability? I'll say.

Chapter 33
Phone Etiquette or "Preoccupation"

• You make a phone call and your customer answers: "Say, can I call you back in five minutes, I'm kind of busy right now." (Well, I guess that's better than call waiting.) I'm left to wonder: Why did they pick up the phone in the first place?

• You call your customer and one of their kids answers. (For best results use kids between ten and sixteen years old.)

Scenario one:

"Is your dad or mom home?"

"No."

"Can you leave a message?"

"Sure."

"Okay…(Insert message) Thanks."

Results: No return call from either mom or dad.

Scenario two:

"Is your dad or mom there?"

"No."

"Can you hang up the phone so I can call back and leave a message on the recorder?"

"Sure."

Results: Dad or mom returns your call.

• You know your customer doesn't really want to talk to you in person when they leave a message on the office phone at 7:00 p.m.

• You know somehow they are not going to "get it" when your subcontractor keeps on talking over you without allowing any time for listening:

"Hello?"

"Hi, this is Mick."

"Hi, Mick, could you hold on a second, I'm on another call."

Hmmm, it's nice to feel wanted. (I wait until Jim comes back on the line.)

"Hey, Jim, how's it going?"

"Not bad, Mick, can you call me back in five minutes?"

"Sure."

(I call back in five minutes.)

"This is Jim's voicemail. Please leave a message."

(Some days you just can't win.)

Chapter 34
My Husband Is Christian/Baptist/Atheist/Catholic/Jewish/Italian/_____ (You Fill In the Blank)

Sometimes religion can play a roll in the bidding process. Trusting another customer's intuition cannot be downplayed either. I gave a customer a quote on a master bedroom and bath remodel extension. The quote contained the price and a brief description of the work. I often do this to save the time of writing a detailed proposal.

After she received the quote, Sally asked if she could look at any of our current jobs. I told her I would get permission from some customers to see if they would let her look at their remodel. One of my customers, a very nice lady named Anne, graciously let Sally walk through her kitchen and laundry remodel.

I was not onsite when Sally met Anne, but I saw Anne shortly after their meeting and she wanted to talk to me.

"Mick, oh my gosh, I don't think you should work with that woman."

"Why not, Anne? Didn't she like our work?"

"No, that wasn't it. She loved the work! It was just the questions she asked. Oh, I don't know, something just didn't feel right."

I didn't dwell on the topic with Anne, but thanked her anyway. About a week later, I mailed a proposal to Sally and her husband. Two days later I received a call from Sally asking if we could go over a part of the proposal.

"My husband doesn't like the draw schedule." (That's a schedule of payments, tied to completion of certain portions of the project rather than to dates.)

"What do you mean? What part does he want to change?"

"Well. Please don't tell anyone this, but my husband is [a member of a particular religion] and he thinks the final draw is too small. It should be about $8,000, not $3,000."

This conversation was starting to surprise me; not because they wanted to change the draw schedule, which happens periodically. Sometimes depending on the circumstances I may adjust the payment schedule, but not very often.

Some people just like to be in control or don't feel safe unless they have what they believe is leverage. There are a lot of horror stories about contractors taking payments and then walking off the job; or shoddy workmanship. So in a way I can't blame them.

No, the surprise is I have never heard anyone try to manipulate a draw schedule based on his or her faith, or lack thereof. I have worked with people of many faiths and I try to treat them as I myself would like to be treated. I have found that there are good and bad people of all religious persuasions. Thankfully, there's always more good ones than bad.

This couple's attempt at manipulation was, for me, a red flag; the kind a bull sees before he aims his big horns in my direction.

"I'm sorry," I said, "but I can't change the draw schedule."

"Why not?"

"Well, let me put it this way. Your last draw is $3,000. If you read the language, at this point we virtually have your job completed, except for any minor touch-up items and a final inspection. The total cost of your job is $90,000. In essence, I'm lending you $90,000 with the hope that you will pay us after we have already completed the work for you. So from my point of view, you're already in the driver's seat."

To make a long story short, I didn't take this project—for more than the reasons outlined above. This couple became angry with me and accused someone in our office of incompetence after they received their plans back. Sally called and left a message saying some idiot put the plans in a flowerpot full of water. I'm the idiot who brought the plans back and tucked them safely between their flowerpot and front door.

No, the main reason I did not take on this project is something that has taken me twenty-five years to learn, and am in fact still trying to learn. There has to be communication between the contractor and the homeowners. More importantly both the husband and the wife have to be on the same page, involved, show interest in the project, and communicate together.

Looking back in time I have seen a handful of projects go wrong for whatever reason, be it money, time, stress, etc., or either the husband or the wife does not want the project to go forward. The trick is to ascertain this before you enter into a contract with the couple.

A contractor can't afford to "take sides"—or be the football. In other words, get kicked around.

Chapter 35
Don't You Have Any Bad News You'd Like to Share?

Gary worked for a large corporation in the Bay Area. His wife also commuted to San Francisco, so they both traveled a lot. They also went to corporate "black tie" events from time to time due to his company obligations.

Even with their busy schedules, together we were able to complete what amounted to a whole house remodel; including a new section on one side of the kitchen, remodeling three bathrooms, a new study/office, a beautiful coffered ceiling, and a new fireplace mantle in the family room.

Lynn, Gary's wife, handled most of the day-to-day decisions and it was a pleasure to work with her. When their house was complete, it was a showplace which, from time to time, we were able to show to potential customers.

Months after we finished this project, Lynn called me and asked us to complete a few more small projects, which we did. We caught up on each others' lives, and she mentioned her experience while attending a corporate party hosted by the company her husband works for.

"The biggest surprise of the party was the fact that many of the people there were telling stories about their remodels."

"You're kidding! It must have been a boring party."

"No, not at all. As a matter of fact, most of the stories had something in common."

"Really? In what way?"

"They were all horror stories."

"Horror stories? What kind of horror stories?"

"Well… One woman told me her contractor started her kitchen over six months ago and is nowhere close to being finished."

"Wow! That's no horror story, that's a nightmare!"

"It sure is. Anyway a few other women gathered around to hear this woman's story and pretty soon three or four other women shared similar stories. One lady even said her contractor abandoned the job. That's horrible."

"It sure is. Those kind of stories don't help anyone, contractors included."

"After listening to all those depressing stories, I decided to share my own experience." Lynn then looked at me expectantly.

"Well, I hope your story wasn't a tale of woe."

Lynn smiled at me and said, "No, but you're not going to believe the response I got."

"What kind of response?" I asked, eager to hear the ending of a story I had participated in.

"Well, I proceeded to tell them about our remodel and how wonderfully it turned out. I described our beautiful kitchen, the spectacular coffered ceiling, the gorgeous cabinets surrounding the television, and our incredible master bath."

"And what did they say?"

"The woman who told that first story said she bet the job ran way over schedule. 'On the contrary,' I told them, 'the project was completed on time and pretty close to our original budget. The same contractor was just at my house again remodeling my study.'"

I smiled. "What did they say to that?"

"They all had shocked looks on their faces! And disappointment, I think."

I shook my head . Unfortunately, I guess it's true: Misery loves company. That, and no one likes a boring story. Me? I'll take boring anytime.

Chapter 36
A Tale of the Tails

I'm often called to a customer's home to give them a bid on termite or dry rot damage. Sometimes a couple will call me to look over a house they want to buy. The first question they want answered is: "Is the place worth it?" Some of these couples don't have faith in the home inspectors sent to inspect the house by their realtors.

When looking over these homes I usually crawl underneath the homes into the crawlspaces to check for moisture or cracks. I also climb into the attics to inspect for leaks, structural integrity, and if the attic has adequate insulation. I also walk the outside of the house carefully, checking for dry rot or termite damage.

I carry a five-foot steel probe with a sharp point as I walk around the house. With the probe I can reach up and inspect single-story rafters and beams. If the probe "sticks" to the wood ands does not penetrate, usually the lumber is sound. If it penetrates and starts going through the wood like it's butter, then what I have probably found is dry rot; wood that has been damaged by water contact.

A lot of times this damage occurs because the house has not been maintained properly. A good example of this would be gutters clogged with leaves. When it rains, the gutters fill up and often push the water up to the underside of the roof sheeting. This often starts the process of decay under the roof material and sometimes on the rafters. The rafters are wood members that support the roof.

Or, on the weather side of the house if the wood siding is allowed to be exposed too long to the elements without a fresh coat of paint, whole sheets will eventually lose their structural integrity and start to disintegrate. This process can happen faster than you think. Worse, it can be extremely expensive to repair this type of damage.

I have looked at dozens of homes for clients and after a while you become adept at knowing how to locate potential problems. I make it a habit to periodically walk around my own home also. During one of these walks I found something protruding up through the concrete floor in my garage. If my wife had not been gone that morning I probably wouldn't have noticed it because it was directly below where she parks her car.

At first glance I thought a five-inch-tall pencil was standing on its eraser, upright. In fact, it was a termite tube growing up through the wood expansion joint between two concrete slabs. The tube is shaped like pencil, but a little thinner, and is made from dirt. The termites need the moisture of this tube to survive. (If you see one on a foundation wall outside your home call a termite or pest control company sooner rather than later.)

I hired my painter to power wash and paint the exterior of my home a few years ago in anticipation of selling it. My painter, working on the southeast side of my home called me over. "Look at those rafters."

I looked up under the eave where he pointed. The ends of the rafters looked solid and the existing paint still covered them fairly well. "I don't see anything. What's the problem, Rod?"

He handed me a stepladder and said, "Put your fingers on the end of that rafter tail."

I climbed up and grabbed a hold of the end of the two-by-four rafter tail, which looked solid. My fingers went right through it. The only part of the rafter that had maintained its integrity was the paint that coated it.

I was shocked, especially since I thought I paid attention to my house. Apparently, I am more thorough with my customers than I am with my own home. Fortunately only the tail ends of the rafter were rotten, necessitating repairs costing around $300.

Chapter 37
The Pointer Sisters

We usually have several crews working simultaneously on different jobs during the course of any given day. On one of these jobs two of my brothers were framing the walls for a new master bedroom. They were at the stage where they had to raise a heavy beam, which was going to sit on the top of the new walls.

The framing was taking place at the rear of the house, too far to reach with a crane. My brother Tony called me and asked for some more manpower to raise the beam by hand. I called Steve and Shawn, another crew working on a job three miles away.

Steve and Shawn arrived at my brother's job and listened to some directions on how they were going to raise the beam. As they moved into position Steve said, "Where's the pointers?"

"Pointers?" Tom asked.

"Yeah, the pointers, you know." Steve poses with one hand on his hip, and the other pointing to where the beam was going to sit.

"Who are the pointers?" Tony asked wondering if Steve meant Tom and himself.

"John and Lewis," Steve said proudly as Shawn snickered.

Apparently they all had a good laugh over this even though Steve seemed sincere in his presentation. Later as my brothers related the story to me, we also laughed until I realized this might not be as funny as it seems.

On John's job the next day, Tiny, another employee, had also heard about the pointers. He even came up with a nickname for them, "Twisted Sisters," named after some punk band.

I said, "I have a better name. How about the Pointer Sisters?" Tiny laughed with glee. He walked up to John and asked if he knew who the Pointer Sisters were? Feigning ignorance, John said he didn't.

"You know, the pointers," Tiny said as he pointed his finger towards the wall John was working on. John's face flushed, finally realizing what Tiny was talking about. It was a shame that Lewis was gone at that moment, picking up some materials. I'm sure he would have enjoyed Tiny's story also.

Ironically, prior to hearing the Pointer Sister story, Lewis and John had been working alone on the same job for two weeks.

This left me wondering about the state of their job and the progress they were making. After all with two pointers on the same job, was either one of them actually getting any work done?

Inadvertently, this may have served as a wake-up call for John and Lewis, although in their defense, progress was evident on their job. It seems they only brought out their pointers when Steve and Shawn were working on the same job with them.

Chapter 38
Hurrah for the Good Customer

Sometimes, especially when comparing stories, it's easy to forget all the great customers we have worked with over the years. The customers that have been difficult may in reality be a fraction of one percent, yet the tendency is to dwell on that minuscule number. And that would not be fair to the vast majority who support us. The "good customer" is the reason we have not used Yellow Pages advertisements for years. Our first group of good customers have given us many referrals to more good customers.

Good customers are as motivated as the contractor to see their project through to a successful completion. The good customer understands the value of having professionals work on their jobs since more than likely the customer is a professional in his or her own field.

I like to think that no matter what the situation is, compromise is always possible. There are, however, the few that are the exception. These people may possibly be the reason that there are so many lawyers and paralegals in our state. These people seem to be looking for a lawsuit before they have even met you. We have all run into people who seem to feed on conflict. There is no way to reason with them. Fortunately, in the almost twenty-five years I have been on my own, I have never taken a residential customer to a court of law.

I can count on my one hand the customers that have left a bad taste in my mouth. Ironically, except for one divorced woman, they were all couples that appeared to have some emotional problems. Since I realize I should focus on what I know, I won't presume to elaborate on my limited knowledge of the human psyche. Suffice it to say that there is a pattern here!

That's enough negativity. There is also a pattern when dealing with the good customer. It is so subtle that sometimes it is hard to remember these people as readily, and that would be a terrible shame, because these are the people I am grateful for. I happen to believe that given the chance, most of us are kind, decent human beings ... So once again, thanks to all our customers.

Chapter 39
My Cats Don't Pee in the House
or Who's in Charge?

"*My* cats don't pee in the house!" I must have heard this phrase over a dozen times, and each time I hear it, it is obvious the owner believes it with all their heart. I carry a black light in my truck because when you shine it over the carpet, an unmistakable crystal color pattern becomes evident. This color change shows on anything covered in animal urine.

We were in one customer's house preparing to make some repairs when it became painfully apparent that no black light would be needed to locate "hidden" urine. My brother Joe and I walked into the house and were immediately bombarded with a pungent cat odor. The odor was so strong it hurt our eyes. I, for one, had to breathe through my mouth. My brother looked at me and briefly held his nose. No discussion was necessary, especially when oxygen was in such short supply.

The woman who answered the door seemed to be breathing fine and seemed oblivious to the acrid stench. As she walked us through the house I counted at least ten cats. The house itself was built on a golf course in a beautiful neighborhood. I guessed that sans the cat problems, the house had to be worth over $800,000.

One of the projects involved removing carpet from three bedrooms and a hallway. The customer left the home while the work was being completed. Joe called me back that afternoon to show me some more problems.

The cat urine was so strong, not only did it ruin all the carpet and padding, but it had also stained the particleboard underlayment sheets under the padding. Removing the carpet and pad did not get rid of the horrible smell, so we decided the floor had to be treated with a product called Kilz, a stain blocker and sealer.

The biggest surprise we found was in the master bedroom. Joe had already removed the carpet. He pointed to spot in the floor where the particleboard was actually eaten through by the acidity of the cat urine. Joe explained that the spot was right at the side of the bed.

It didn't take long to figure out how that happened. Apparently, one or more of the cats slept on the bed with this woman. When the cats had to relieve themselves in the middle of the night, they simply jumped off the side of the bed, relieved themselves on the floor, then hopped back into bed and continued sleeping in luxury.

How these people could not know all this is beyond my comprehension. Don't get me wrong. I love pets. We have three dogs ourselves. I understand we are creatures of habit that continually learn to adapt, but this takes it to a new level. The cost of the damage was high, but after being in that house for a short period of time, the issue of our health became paramount. As my brother Joe told me, "Mick, never again!" I concur.

Chapter 40
A Lesson from the Teacher

Years ago, in our second year working together, my brothers and I learned a valuable lesson ... from a teacher no less. Ironically, he was our first repeat customer. The year before we did some work for Steve and everything worked out nicely.

This time around the job was larger, consisting of a bath remodel, some interior trim, drywall, and wall texture repairs. Once again I presented Steve with a fairly detailed contract, which he signed.

We witnessed an incident during this time that should have raised a very large red flag, but unfortunately went unheeded. Sears delivered a large television for Steve and his wife. As they carried it down the stairs the top of the television nicked the ceiling, causing minor damage to the drywall. Unseemly words like "lawsuit," "my attorney," "you're paying for the damages," and "we expect a new TV," spewed from Steve and Carol's mouths. We never learned how this incident turned out, but looking back I can make an educated guess.

The following week, Steve had a garage sale and somehow sold his washer and dryer, which were in use at the time. Steve asked my brother Tony if we could build some platforms in the laundry room for a new European state-of-the-art washer and dryer, and also build a

Formica folding counter over the units. He pleaded with Tony, saying his family could not do without a washer and dryer.

I worked out a price based on what Tony told me, which Steve accepted. I was on another job that week about an hour away. Steve seemed like a reasonable person, so we started the work without getting a signed change order from him. I figured I could have him sign one later. As life often does, other thoughts and concerns permeated my mind and I forgot all about the change order.

The job was completed the following week and, as was my custom in those early years, I met Steve in person to present the final bill and to look over our work. When I arrived, Steve was already holding a check in his hand. We walked the job site finding everything in order.

I handed him the final invoice. He briefly glanced at it and handed me the check.

I looked at it and quickly determined that it was the full contract amount, without the $900 for the additional work he had requested. Here is a loose translation of our conversation:

"Steve, is everything completed to your satisfaction?"

"Yes, it is, Mick. Thanks for a great job."

"I couldn't help noticing that it appears you didn't pay for the change order."

"That's correct."

"Did you ask for the additional work to be completed?"

"Yes, I sure did."

"Was the work performed to your satisfaction?"

"Yes it was," he stated matter-of-factly.

"Then can I ask why you didn't pay for that part of your bill?"

"Sure, your contract states that any additional work requires a signed change order. We don't have one."

"Let me get this straight. You're saying you asked for the extra work, you agreed to the price, and the work was done to your satisfaction. (Voice rising ever so slightly.) You just don't feel like paying it. Does that pretty much sum it up?"

"That about covers it."

To make another long story short, I asked him what kind of teacher he was. When he told me, I was fortunate not to have any kids being taught by him, his high moral values notwithstanding. Oh, and he should also be "ashamed of himself."

He wasn't, of course. No remorse. Just self-satisfaction. He was also right. By the letter of the law and contractor's law codes, I should have given him a change order to sign. Unfortunately, trust is sometimes not enough in this business. A paper trail is necessary for the "teachers" of this world. One can only hope this man uses a higher code of ethics with his students.

Chapter 41
I Think I'll Try On-Line Banking

Many years ago, when economical conditions caused by complications affected the cash flow of our fledgling business, I had to make more trips to the bank to make deposits than I care to recall.

On one such trip I had a nasty flu. It was Friday, I was dizzy and nauseous, and had no business being out of bed, except for the fact that the thought of a bounced check would have brought me a different kind of pain.

That is why I sat in my truck on that cold afternoon filling out a deposit slip while seeing double, instead of walking in the bank and handling this business at the counter. I sat in the parking lot for what seemed like minutes, constantly losing my train of thought and starting all over again.

Finally, I got out of my truck and walked through the front glass swinging door. As I stood there adjusting to the light, I noticed a woman lying on the floor, face-down, almost against the counter. My first incoherent thought was that the woman was playing a joke on the teller.

That's when I noticed movement in my peripheral vision. On the teller's side of the counter I saw one man, then another. The second man was pointing a large gun at me.

I reacted before I could process my next thought. I ducked and spun around, grabbing the door in one motion. I yanked the door open, spun left, and ran hard, zigzagging towards a strip mall and a phone booth. It's amazing what adrenaline will do for you!

I thought about looking for a quarter to call 911 and started searching my pockets. I looked back over my shoulder after running about fifty feet in time to see the two hoodlums running out of the door in my direction. I was amazed at my bad luck. Then, just as suddenly, they turned left and were gone.

The following Monday, my fever had broken and I went back to the bank to conduct business. I knew all the tellers there and wanted to see what happened.

"Hi, Jill. You know I walked right in on that bank robbery."

"We know all about it." She giggled as another teller walked up.

"How could you possibly know? I didn't even see you guys. Were you all on the floor?"

The other teller, Susan, burst out laughing. "We saw the whole thing on video. We didn't know you could run so fast!"

I'm glad I was able to ease their pain. I found out later the two lowlifes had been busy. This was their third bank in the area. I heard they only got a few hundred dollars, wisely choosing not to hang around.

Chapter 42
The Seven-Year Itch, Uh, Niche

Finding your niche in this business can be the key to a successful career or one that just plods along, with no clear goals. The trick is to find what you do well and then focus on that aspect.

Contractors in general seem to have a mentality that goes hand in hand with the feast or famine theory. We remember the slow times or the weeks with bad stretches of weather, and worry about where our next job is coming from. I've heard it said that we're one job away from the unemployment line and in our formative years that was very true. Some contractors put too much emphasis on this and therefore sign up every job that comes down the pike.

This can create several problems. Of the two that spring immediately to mind, the first is physics. If you sign up three large kitchen remodels that are all supposed to start in May and you only have three employees, it doesn't take a rocket scientist to see you will not have enough manpower to handle these jobs simultaneously, much less at a level of quality the customer deserves.

The second problem occurs when a contractor bids every job opportunity he or she comes in contact with, regardless of the location and more importantly, the type of work it entails. If your men, for example, are used to installing wood crown and pre-hung doors in nice homes, taking backyard fence jobs may not be in your best interest.

It may take some patience, but once you find your niche and you are well past the learning curve, you will create demand for your chosen field. Customers will seek you out. And finally, your employees just might be happier people.

Chapter 43
Oh Brother

My brothers' names you may have noticed have been sprinkled liberally throughout many of these stories. As I look back on the stages of my life I realize my brothers were there with me, sharing the trials, the tribulations, the successes.

Tony, Tom, and I have worked together continuously for over twenty-four years; and my brothers Vince, Ralph, Joe, and Chris have each worked with us for long stretches at various times. Presently Joe is still a valuable member of our team. It's a sign of our longevity, I guess, that we have the sons of Tony and Joe working on our jobs from time to time to earn spending money.

Another generation. (sigh) Where did all the time go? It passes by much too quickly and must not be squandered.

I may be guilty of taking my brothers for granted from time to time. I love them all—and I think they know that—but I need to slow down periodically and socialize with them more. I need to actually *tell them* how important they are to me.

I wonder if I pass along to them all the compliments we receive from our customers about their work and personalities. Or, how many people specifically request them for jobs. I believe the finest compliment of all is simple: without these men I would not want to attempt to build this business all over again. People like them are rare and very hard to find.

My brothers all benefited from my father's guidance, knowledge, and high moral values. He was the person we all used as a role model, and for him I am truly thankful.

Chapter 44
What Kind of Animal Did This?

Over a decade ago we were remodeling a beautiful home on the Sacramento River. A deck ran alongside the whole west face of the house, affording a breathtaking view of the river. The owner of this home was a direct contradiction to this tranquil area. He was loud and boisterous and usually got what he wanted. He also happened to be a very fair guy and we were fast friends up until the time he died, just recently.

During that remodel, I had an employee named Roger. A nice enough guy although a little rough around the edges, he was also very talkative and prone to large quantities of embellishment. On the plus side, he was an above-average worker.

We were working upstairs on the main floor installing three-and-one-quarter-inch-tall oak base in the kitchen over new ceramic tile. Roger went downstairs to get a rasp. A few minutes later I heard Jack, the owner, bellowing; although all I could make out was my name.

I got up and walked outside onto the deck. I could hear Jack's voice clearer now. It was coming from ground level, under the deck, near the garage. "Get the hell down here, Mick. You won't believe this shit!" he roared. I ran downstairs fearing anything and everything.

"Look at this shit!" Jack was pointing to a pile of firewood leaning against the garage wall. Roger stood a few steps away averting his gaze.

I stared at the woodpile seeing nothing of significance. Deciding to be a wise guy I said, "What? Oh, I see it now. The left side of the pile is crooked. So what!" This further incensed Jack, so I wiped the smile off my face.

"What kind of animal pisses on my house?" the volume of Jack's words was incredible. If he wasn't so angry I would have been tempted to laugh out loud. Instead I looked over at Roger, expecting an explanation.

He shrugged. "It was just on the firewood." That's when I saw the wet patch in the middle of the pile.

Jack didn't miss a beat. "I pick this shit up with my hands!" I was barely holding it in as Jack continued, "What the hell's the matter with you, Roger? You walked right by two bathrooms on the way down here."

Roger said nothing.

Jack continued his tirade, waving broadly at the lines of dampness. "Look at this shit, he was using his tool like a little wand. What kind of animals you got working for you?"

"I had to go," Roger said weakly, all his piss and vinegar apparently drained.

I'll never know what makes some people tick. Maybe it was his way at getting back at society. Maybe he just had the urge to go. I'll never know. What I do know is this, for the next ten years whenever Jack brought up this incident it was as if he was blaming me.

Go figure.

Chapter 45
Who Lives Here Anyway?

One of our customers habitually brought some of her friends over to her house while we were remodeling her kitchen. Most of their comments were of the positive variety.

Invariably though, people have their opinions and some of them will verbalize these thoughts, regardless of the consequences. (Some people just can't help themselves. I call this the "Keeping up with the Joneses syndrome.")

Some comments I have heard include: "I can't believe you picked that color," "Are you sure blue granite is going to work for you?", "You know Suzie has cherry cabinets too; but hers are a shade lighter and they look great," and "I think stainless steel would go better with your décor." Seemingly innocent comments, all with the power to throw a project into turmoil, create customer consternation or indecisiveness, or, at the least, set off a series of panic and/or anxiety attacks in the customer's chest and frontal lobe. Being just the contractor, I usually escape with a minor headache.

Besides the contractor and the owner, three others are usually involved with remodel projects. One is called the architect, the second is the designer, and the third is called common sense.

I personally don't mind a little outside input once in a while, but after the combined effort of many people involved in color and project choices, not to mention scheduling and performing the actual tasks, there comes a time when you have to ask the customer a question: "Is he/she going to be living in the house with you?" If not, it's time to make your choice and finish the project.

Chapter 46
Gung-Ho!

Every once in a while we get an enthusiastic employee with a gung-ho attitude. We like that and generally don't discourage such behavior. One particularly rambunctious employee shall remain nameless, but his story must be told.

We were at our customer's house, doing the preliminary work necessary to convert a rear patio into kitchen space under an existing roof. The patio was six feet deep, and the concrete in this area had to be removed so we could pour a new footing and concrete slab.

Where the roofline and the house wall ended, a concrete deck extended out approximately twenty-five feet and ended at a beautiful in-ground pool. When I met the men that morning I spoke to "X," "Y," and "Z"; although by mannerism and eye contact (and by order of seniority) it was evident that I was giving my instructions to "X."

I stopped by the job a little after lunch and the guys were putting on their tools and walking towards the backyard. When I turned the corner my throat constricted and my stomach filled with butterflies that could only have been created from stress. Not only had the men chopped up all the concrete for the addition, but they had also chopped an additional fifteen feet towards the pool.

I was beside myself. I wonder how far they would have gone had

I not shown up. I asked "X" what he thought he was doing. In short, he claimed that because "Y" and "Z" were listening to me too, they were also responsible. I asked him, "Out of curiosity, were you going to stop at the pool?" What I wanted to say was, *"Weren't you listening to me? Do you realize how much this is going to cost to replace?"* Spreading the blame was not exactly what I was looking for. Instead I made a mental note to give this particular crew more detail and less delegation of authority. You can safely assume that the next time the slab would be marked clearly with paint.

P.S.: The owners were happy with their new concrete patio as well as their new kitchen extension.

Chapter 47
A Window with a View

Several years ago, we were working on an elaborate bath addition which included a spa and glass blocks, with indirect lighting behind it. The elderly gentleman we were doing the work for asked for several additional things to be done around his home—a common occurrence.

One request was to add a window in his master bedroom wall. On this particular wall there were already some windows and the room had plenty of other natural lighting.

(Sometimes a customer's ideas don't make much sense. I remember a woman who wanted a set of swinging French doors where her sliding glass door was located in her dining room. When I told her that the sliding door made more sense because of the space limitations at the dining table, she refused to believe me and went ahead with the project anyway. Three weeks after completion, she called and we came and removed the French doors and put in a brand-new sliding door. Now back to our window story.)

I told the customer that I did not think adding this window made any sense, especially considering the additional cost involved and the fact that he would be losing more valuable wall space.

He was adamant, however, so in the following weeks a new window was installed while my crews worked on the bathroom. When

I checked on the work, it became apparent why the owner wanted this window in this particular location.

The house next door was rented to four female college students who were generously given access to our customer's outdoor hot tub whenever they wanted. From the acute angle where I now stood in my customer's bedroom, I finally "saw the light." The customer's request made much more sense, at least as it pertained to him.

Chapter 48
The Case of the Paralegal and the Missing Panties

This story brings to mind how much fun it is to live and work in a college town. We do a lot of work in apartments where many students reside and sometimes it's easy to spot which ones are in law school. Some of these kids are practicing law while they are still in diapers, so to speak. I like to call this group the "Para-Legals." My brother Joe had some firsthand experience with one of them.

Joe was sent to an apartment complex to change out some windowsills. The majority of the tenants were college students. Even if one wasn't aware of this going in, after traipsing through apartments with hundreds of empty beer cans, people sleeping all over the floor while the sun was shining, and navigating through piles of smelly clothes; it became painfully evident.

The apartment manager received a call the next morning, which she graciously shared with me. It seemed that Joe was being accused of moving and playing with some of the girls' panties. (They were not wearing them at the time. These were garments strewn all over the floor, some in the proximity of the windows Joe worked on.)

They couldn't have accused a worse candidate of being a pervert. Joe is a family man, active in his church, and will not even tolerate foul language. There has never been a customer complaint about him in the fifteen years he has been with our company.

What the girls attempted next though, was a surprise. The girls threatened litigation and then threatened to move out. When they finished blowing smoke and the dust finally settled, all they really wanted was what many attorneys of the ambulance chasing variety try to get: a reduction in rent. What they should have asked for was some washing detergent and a maid.

Case closed!

Chapter 49
The Letter of the Law

Many small towns that we work in have unusual ways of enforcing the law. A recent example had to do with working in the basement of a police station in their core downtown area.

The job was difficult in a number of ways, not the least of which was parking. On-street parking was practically nonexistent, and most of it was limited to just two hours. There was also no place to keep our materials and tools, unless we wanted to risk losing them.

Essentially, the guys had to move their trucks every two hours to keep from getting ticketed. (I should mention that I did not try to get any type of parking permits; nor did the city police who hired us offer any. In hindsight, we should have asked for temporary permits. But I digress.)

The first day passed uneventfully, except for the additional time wasted carting tools back and forth and moving vehicles. Not to mention searching for parking spaces. On day two we received parking tickets on two vehicles which had our company logo on them. On day three, we got an additional ticket.

At $35 a pop, I finally had my fill. Just above from where we were doing the actual work, was the first-floor office where citations were handled. As I carried all my tickets up the flight of stairs, I had a flight of fantasy, a fleeting vision of the officer on duty tearing up the tickets, apologizing, and quickly sending me on my merry way.

Unfortunately the only part of my daydream that came true was how quickly they got rid of me. To summarize their comments, "Why didn't you get a temporary parking permit?"

"Gee, I don't know. Maybe because I was doing some work for the police!" No sympathy; I paid up.

I wonder if I can build fines into my budget?

Chapter 50
Why Me?

• *"I'm going to be sick …" (and it's best I tell you when you're not in)*
I'm busy doing paperwork and writing proposals at my desk one morning at five o'clock. It's quiet; and without constant phone-ringing I can accomplish a great deal of work. Then the phone rings. It's 5:02. I let the machine pick it up. One of my employees is on the line. "Mick, I'm not feeling too good…" (Spoken with an appropriate hint of suffering.) "I think I'll need the day off. If I feel better, I'll come in in the afternoon." (Did I mention it's Monday morning? Enough said.)

• *Pass it on…*
I walk into a customer's home to prepare to give them a bid. The husband and wife both shake my hand. Then the wife says, "Be careful. Don't get near us or the kids. We're all in the midst of some kind of virus … You know, the crud that's going around." (Thanks… a lot.)

• *(and, on the subject of fads…) Are two heads better than one?*
"Mick, I saw this picture in a magazine, where they have two opposing shower heads. What do you think?" Janna says, holding out a clipping.

"Well, assuming your existing copper pipe running to the bath is three-quarter-inch, installing that shouldn't be a problem. What does Harry think about this idea?"

"He doesn't seem to be too excited about it, to tell you the truth."

"Well," I tell her, "we're not romantic spring chickens anymore." I usually ask the customer what the main reason is for making a change. "So, do you think you would actually use both heads simultaneously?" (Long pause.)

Today, Janna is extremely happy with one tall showerhead for her husband and a slide arm beside it holding a smaller head to use with the shower seat, for washing hair, or to clean the shower.

Function before style … Works every time.

Chapter 51
Bizarro World

Sometimes there is just no rhyme or reason for a customer's logic. Until you know *why* they believe what they are saying is true, you have to roll with the punches. Some customers' expectations—or accusations—defy any reasonable explanation. Here are some cases in point:

• We have been blamed for broken sewer lines under concrete slabs, when suds from a laundry load were seen coming through a crack in the sidewalk, even though no work was performed on this particular sewer line.

• I have given free advice for observations before, and then been threatened with litigation.

• A customer once accused us of mixing oil-based paint with water-based paint and then painting her interior walls with this concoction. (I'm fairly certain that oil and water do not mix.) If tried, the coagulated mess left on the walls would not be smooth, let alone pretty.

• Another customer believed we caused cracks in her drywall *three rooms away* from where we were completing a bath remodel. (I investigated these cracks and found dust and grime in them that was probably from the Vietnam War era.) To add insult to injury, this same customer implied that while we were using the garage door leading into her home, we broke her doorknob. (The knob looked to be about thirty-five years old—older than I was at the time—and clearly had been on its last leg.)

I'm sure some of these people sincerely believed some of these assertions and many more just like them. Quite possibly, for instance, the doorknob did finally give out the day we were there—on the 25,550th time it was used! Anything is possible. (Sometimes things just wear out and break.) In fairness to our customers, I would always expect my employees to report to me immediately any breakage or unfortunate occurrences on the job site; but, human nature being what it is, that may not always be the case.

It just seems that some people automatically say, "The contractor was here earlier, he must have done this."

At some point during conversations of this type, I half expect an audience to start clapping as Geraldo Rivera comes onstage to perpetrate his ruse on an unsuspecting contractor.

Some of these incidents remind me of a conversation George and Jerry had on a Seinfeld episode, in which they discuss a world where everything has turned upside down and functions the exact opposite of what you expected. "Bizarro World" they called it. As I recall, Superman may have had something to do with it. This is the world I currently occupy.

There's a reason I am bringing up all this unpleasantness.

In all the years our company has been in business, we have never taken a customer to court to solve our problems. (Once, we were involved in an arbitration which was, in itself, an interesting chapter in my life. One I hope not to repeat in the near future.)

We live in an increasingly litigious society, where people are ready to sue each other at the drop of a hat. But I'm still an optimist.

I believe that if people communicate with each other, and are willing to work with each other with mutual respect, then most, if not all, problems can be solved without any ill will. Or bringing anyone into a courtroom.

For a general contractor, as well as for a customer, listening is as important as the art of speaking. If not more so. Of course many problems can be avoided with detailed plans and a clear concise contract. I believe that most people are inherently good. And we all deserve a chance to prove it.

Chapter 52
Don't Let the Door Hit You on the Way Out

Up until a few years ago, my father worked on some of our projects as a working foreman. He was sixty-eight years old at the time and still he could keep up with or outwork many of the younger guys.

He also had a propensity for weeding out employees who were slackers or otherwise not inclined to put in a full day's work for a full day's wages; which brings me to the story of an employee who recently worked with my father.

My father and several of our full-time employees were working on an apartment project, replacing sheets of siding on the first- and second-floor walls. The job entailed the replacement of over two hundred sheets including trim and was going to last several weeks. I decided to hire a temporary employee to help with this project.

Dan, a forty-one-year-old man, showed up on the job the following Monday, on time. On my visits to the job everyone seemed to be performing their jobs adequately. The first sign of any friction occurred when Dan walked into my office on Friday afternoon, about one hour before quitting time.

"What's up, Dan?"

"I can't work for that hardass anymore!"

"Who are you talking about, Dan?"

"Domenic. He's all over my case."

"Well, what's the problem?"

"He won't let us finish our breaks, and if you're a couple of minutes late, he's all over our butts, plus he's working us like crazy!"

I thought about this for a moment. "You know, Dan, that 'hardass' you're talking about is my father and he's sixty-eight years old. You should be ashamed of yourself."

As a side note, after speaking with my father, I found out Dan was showing up ten minutes late, and rolling up his tools early. On top of that he showed an aversion to work and disappeared for minutes on end somewhere within the apartment complex, ostensibly to relieve himself or to find a tool he needed. It should be noted that none of the other men complained about my father. We were all happy to have his vast knowledge and expertise at our disposal.

Since this wasn't the first time, I thanked my father for weeding out another irritant so quickly. Sometimes these irritants can fester for weeks before they are rooted out.

About the Author

Michael Pesola was born in New York City in 1957, the second oldest of twelve children. He moved to California in 1973.

He is a second-generation general contractor, currently doing business in northern California. He owns Bedrock Construction along with his brothers Paul and Dom Pesola.

Michael completed his bachelor of business degree at National University. He successfully completed an Institute of Children's Literature course and was published in *Highlights for Children*. He has also written *The Bedrock Guide to Remodeling Success*, a book that prepares customers for the remodel process.

Michael lives in Davis, California, with his wife Sara and their three dogs.

Printed in the United States
95796LV00005B/49-54/A